Henry Morris

Early History of Springfield

An address delivered October 16, 1875 - on the two hundredth

anniversary of the burning of the town by the Indians

Henry Morris

Early History of Springfield
An address delivered October 16, 1875 - on the two hundredth anniversary of the burning of the town by the Indians

ISBN/EAN: 9783337368685

Printed in Europe, USA, Canada, Australia, Japan

Cover: Foto ©Andreas Hilbeck / pixelio.de

More available books at **www.hansebooks.com**

1636—1675.

Early History of Springfield.

AN

ADDRESS

Delivered October 16, 1875,

ON THE

Two Hundredth Anniversary

OF THE

BURNING OF THE TOWN BY THE INDIANS.

BY

HENRY MORRIS.

—

WITH AN APPENDIX.

SPRINGFIELD, MASS.:
F. W. MORRIS, Publisher.
1876.

CLARK W. BRYAN & CO.,
PRINTERS AND BINDERS,
SPRINGFIELD, MASS.

SPRINGFIELD, June 10, 1875.

Hon. HENRY MORRIS:

Dear Sir,—As citizens of Springfield, we think it important that the prominent events in the early history of the town should be kept in remembrance, with such fullness of detail as is possible, and wish to have the benefit of your familiarity with the subject in putting into permanent form an account of the burning of the town, about two hundred years ago, by the Indians. Will you, therefore, make a public address, on such day as shall seem to you appropriate, concerning the occurrence above named, and oblige

Yours respectfully,

A. L. SOULE,	E. WIGHT,
S. G. BUCKINGHAM,	D. H. BRIGHAM,
HENRY BREWER,	R. HATHAWAY,
JAMES BREWER,	BENJAMIN HANNIS,
TITUS AMIDON,	J. S. CARR,
JOEL KENDALL,	HENRY F. TRASK,
LEWIS WARRINER,	HORACE WHEELER,
N. A. LEONARD,	E. S. STACY,
H. N. TINKHAM,	M. P. KNOWLTON,

W. L. SMITH.

SPRINGFIELD, June 16, 1875.

Messrs. A. L. SOULE, S. G. BUCKINGHAM, and others:

Gentlemen,—In the hope that I may contribute something to the stock of knowledge of the early history of this town, and particularly in regard to an event of so much importance as the burning of the town by the Indians in 1675, I accept your invitation to deliver an historical address upon the anniversary of that transaction. The Indians fixed the day, two hundred years ago, on the 5th of October (O. S.), which corresponds to October 16th of the present calendar. The place and hour, I leave to you.

Very respectfully,

HENRY MORRIS.

PREFACE.

———•••———

I HAVE in my possession a printed copy of a sermon, from the title-page of which it appears to have been "delivered in the First Parish in Springfield on the 16th of October, 1775, just one hundred years from the burning of the town by the Indians. By Robert Breck, A. M., pastor of the church there."

Upon receiving the invitation printed on a previous page, it seemed to me that the precedent of 1775 might properly be followed in 1875, and so I consented to undertake the task.

I do not claim for this address the merit of being a full history of this town, during the period of time covered by it. Its main purpose is to narrate with as much particularity as possible, the incidents of the Indian assault upon the town. The history of such antecedent events has been given as appeared suitable to introduce the narrative of the catastrophe of October 5, 1675.

In the preparation of this address and the appendix, I have derived information and aid from the following sources:

Massachusetts Colony Records.

History of New England, by John Winthrop.

Hutchinson's History of the Colony of Massachusetts Bay.

Holmes' Annals of America.

Trumbull's History of Connecticut.

Hubbard's Indian Wars.

Drake's History and Biography of the Indians.

Present State of the Indian War, by a Merchant of Boston, edited by S. G. Drake.

Breck's Century Sermon, October 16, 1775.

Rev. Dr. Lathrop's Sermon, August 25, 1796.

Rev. Dr. Sprague's Discourse, December 2, 1824.

Address by Hon. George Bliss, March 24, 1828, at the opening of the Town Hall in Springfield.

Address by Hon. Oliver B. Morris, May 25, 1836, on the two hundredth anniversary of the settlement of Springfield. (Manuscript).

Records kept by William Pynchon and John Pynchon. (Manuscript).

Town Records of Springfield.

Hampden County Records of Deeds.

Savage's Genealogical Dictionary.

Mather's Magnalia.

Travels in New England, by Timothy Dwight, late President of Yale College.

Foot's History of Brookfield.

Haven's History of Dedham.

For the steel plate, from which the portrait of William Pynchon has been printed, I am indebted to the courtesy of his descendant, Dr. Joseph C. Pynchon of this city.

H. M.

Springfield, December 1, 1875.

Historical Address.

THE BURNING OF SPRINGFIELD.

———•••———

THE march of emigration in the years 1635 and 1636 from the cluster of settlements that fringed Massachusetts Bay, westward to the valley of the Connecticut, was, under the circumstances of that time, a movement of extraordinary boldness. We, who step into spacious and elegant cars, and sit down in cushioned seats, and, while we read the news of the day, are borne in three short hours from the Bay to the river, hardly conscious of the passage, so rapidly and comfortably made, can form no idea of what it was for our fathers to set out upon their journey of one hundred miles into the unexplored interior, away from friends and neighbors, through trackless forests, over rugged hills and mountains, across unbridged streams and swamps, with no guide but the sun and the compass, in peril by day from savage men, and from savage beasts at night. One large party of these emigrants, which reached the Connecticut near the mouth of the Scantic in East Windsor, was fourteen days on the journey. Other parties accomplished the journey in a shorter time.

When the emigrants reached their destination they were without homes to welcome them to their shelter. Houses were to be built, the ground was to be broken up and prepared for cultivation, and the necessaries of life to be provided. All this work was to be done at a distance from civilized neighbors so great, that, however pressing the need, no resort could be had to them for help. Their only neighbors were the Indians, whose wigwams and hunting and fishing-grounds were scattered around them. What kind of neighbors these would prove to be, was a problem not then solved. Some indications were unfavorable. Already an English vessel, that had entered the mouth of the river, and was proceeding a short distance up the stream, had been boarded by Indians, who had treacherously murdered the captain and crew, and plundered and sunk the vessel. A general apprehension pervaded the settlements at the bay of danger from the Pequots and other hostile tribes. Stringent orders had been passed by the General Court against the sale of fire-arms and "strong waters" to the Indians. The military forces of the colony were put in training to prepare for an exigency, expected soon to arrive, and commissioners were appointed to whom was entrusted the conduct of the anticipated Indian war.

It was in such a threatening condition of affairs that the early settlements were begun in the Connecticut valley. A company came from Dorchester in 1635, and planted themselves at Windsor, which they at first called, after their old home, Dorchester. The same year a company came from Watertown, and lo-

cated at Wethersfield, calling that place Watertown.
In the year 1636 Hartford was settled by emigrants
from Cambridge, then called Newtown, who at first
gave the same name to that settlement. All these
emigrations were by license of the General Court first
obtained. (In May, 1635, leave was granted to the inhabitants of Roxbury "to remove themselves to any
place they should think meet," provided they should
still continue under the government of the colony of
Massachusetts Bay. Under this authority, William
Pynchon, with seven other men, came to this place
and commenced a settlement. The Indian name of
the place was Agaam or Agawam, a name specially
designating a meadow on the southerly side of the
Agawam river, but applied in a more general way to
the region on both sides of the Connecticut, including
a large part of what is now comprised in the city of
Springfield. All the favorite grounds of the Indians
had their distinctive names, — Longmeadow was Masacksick; the land bordering on Mill river was Us-
quaick; Plainfield and the region about Brightwood
was Nayasset.

Mr. Pynchon was the leading spirit in this enterprise. He had resided in England at a place called
Springfield, near Chelmsford in Essex, and for that
reason probably, the town, by vote in 1640, bestowed the same name upon his new home here.
He was a gentleman of intelligence, enterprise and
wealth. He was one of the original corporators to
whom King Charles the First granted the colony
charter. Under this charter, the government of the
granted territory was vested in a governor, deputy

2

governor, and eighteen assistants. Mr. Pynchon was named as one of the assistants. When the corporation was transferred from England to America, and the government of it placed in the hands of those members, who came to these shores, and settled in the towns about the Massachusetts Bay, Mr. Pynchon located in Roxbury, and was the founder of that town. While residing there, he was for some years the treasurer of the colony, and always an influential person in the management of its affairs. He was a merchant, and, while at Roxbury, was largely engaged in the fur trade, or, as it was oftener called, the beaver trade. In 1632 he engaged to pay £25 a year into the colonial treasury for the privilege of his beaver trade, and continued this payment until 1635, when the General Court remitted one-fifth of this tax, probably because the trade then had become less profitable. It was undoubtedly that he might avail himself of the superior advantages, afforded by the Connecticut and its tributaries, for the prosecution of this trade, that he was induced to abandon his comparatively comfortable home in Roxbury, and plant himself on the banks of our river.

With Mr. Pynchon came his son-in-law, Henry Smith, Matthew Mitchell, Jehu Burr, William Blake, Edmund Wood, Thomas Ufford and John Cable. These persons, with Mr. Pynchon, were the signers of an agreement bearing date May 14, 1636, intended as a basis for the future regulation of the affairs of the settlement.*

Henry Smith was a gentleman of capacity and cul-

---

* Appendix A.

ture. He was named by the General Court in March, 1636, as one of its commissioners, to administer the government of the settlements on Connecticut River. John Burr was from Roxbury. He was by trade a carpenter. He had been intrusted by the General Court with some important duties while at Roxbury, and, during the two or three years of his residence here, was evidently a person of some consequence. He left Springfield in 1640, and went to Connecticut. John Cable was probably here, at least temporarily, a year or two before Pynchon came. Either in 1634 or 1635 a house of some kind had been built for the anticipated plantation on the west side of the Connecticut, and southerly side of the Agawam, in a meadow, which from that circumstance, was afterwards called the "house-meadow." Cable appears to have been the agent of the plantation in building the house, and he employed one John Woodcock to accompany him from the Bay, and assist in its erection. Cable and Woodcock occupied the house, and the planting ground about it, the same summer. It was probably destroyed or abandoned in the autumn, upon ascertaining that it would be flooded in time of freshets. Cable was the first man who executed the office of constable in this town. He was defendant in the first lawsuit here, of which there is any record. It was an action, brought against him by Woodcock for work done on the house in "house-meadow."*

Matthew Mitchell and William Blake remained here but a very short time. Blake returned to Dorchester, from which town he had come, and Mitchell went

---

* Appendix B.

to Connecticut, where he lived in various towns until
his death.

Four other persons at least soon joined the little
company of settlers, and became with them proprietors
of lots in the plantation. Only three of these twelve
first settlers remained here over three years. But
others came to take the places of those who left.
Houses—rude structures of course at first—were
built, the necessary work of cultivation was begun, and
the foundations of our city were permanently laid.

It was called at first the "Plantation of Agawam,"
and, in the absence of any survey, it was a matter of
question whether it was within the limits of the Massachusetts patent. The General Court, however,
assumed temporary jurisdiction over all the river
plantations, as far south as Wethersfield. When
granting liberty to the inhabitants of the towns bordering on the Massachusetts Bay, whom it styled
"our loving friends, neighbors, freemen, and members," to remove to the river of Connecticut, it appointed eight commissioners, of whom William Pynchon was the second named, and Henry Smith the
fifth, to exercise civil, criminal, and military jurisdiction over the river plantations for one year. Roger
Ludlow, whose name stood first in this commission,
was a resident of Dorchester, and had been deputy
governor of Massachusetts in the year 1634. He settled in Windsor.

The government of the river towns was admin-
istered by this commission for about two years. In
November, 1636, Mr. Pynchon was at Hartford as a
member of the Court then in session there.

In 1638 the question of jurisdiction over the river towns had been substantially adjusted, the Massachusetts authorities retaining the jurisdiction over Springfield, and conceding that over the lower towns to Connecticut. But, before the General Court had made provision for the government of this distant plantation, the planters themselves, on the 14th of February, 1639, in the spirit of genuine democracy, by general consent, agreed and voted " to ordain Mr. William Pynchon to execute the office of a magistrate in this our plantation of Agawam," with ample authority to administer justice with the aid of a jury of six persons, until otherwise directed from the General Court.*

Under this general consent, Mr. Pynchon appears to have exercised all the functions of a magistrate, until in June, 1641, he was duly commissioned by the General Court, with powers similar to those granted by the popular vote.

Any narrative of events, occurring in this town, during the first half century of its existence, will fail to convey to the mind a just and adequate impression of their character, unless we have a tolerably correct conception of the local situation of the town during the same period. This idea is not easily acquired. It is difficult for those who have only known Springfield as a thriving city of thirty thousand inhabitants, its numerous streets crowded with substantial and handsome buildings, both public and private, to appreciate its condition two hundred years ago.

* Appendix C.

During the first fifty years, the dwelling-houses of the town were all on one street, and that the Main street of our time. They were all located on the westerly side of the street. Each householder had a home lot, extending from the street to the river. The major part of these home lots were laid out eight rods wide ; a few were ten, three were fourteen, two were twenty rods, and Mr. Pynchon's thirty rods. The dwelling-houses, standing upon these home lots, were humble structures, compared with the mansions of modern days. With one or two exceptions at the most, they had thatched roofs. Shingled roofs were a rarity in those times, in which but few here could indulge. There is no reason to suppose that there was more than a single brick building here, for more than a century after the first settlement. The chimneys are said to have been wooden frames, covered with mortar, in the early days of the town. To guard against the peculiar exposure to conflagration, resulting from the use of such inflammable materials, every householder was required to be provided with a ladder of sufficient length, and the carrying of fire from house to house, not being sufficiently covered, was made a penal offence.*

Along the easterly margin of the street, ran the brook, called the Garden or Town brook, which, coming down from the high grounds east, divided into two streams at what is now Worthington street, one turning northward, and the other pursuing a southerly course, both ultimately finding their way into the Connecticut. Easterly of this brook, and be-

* Appendix D.

tween it and the upland, was wet, marshy ground, which the early records call the "hasseky marish." Each inhabitant, who had a home lot, had his proportionate share of this marsh opposite his home lot, and of the upland still further east, which was then mostly covered with forest. Besides the Main street, there were three narrow roads or lanes, leading from it westerly to the river. One of these was a road one rod wide, that led to the training-place and burying-ground on the bank of the river. This road, with a greatly increased width, is the Elm street of our day. At the foot of this lane, was the wharf or landing-place, sometimes called the middle wharf. The other two roads to the river are now represented by York and Cypress streets. Of the streets, now running easterly from Main street, State street is much the most ancient. It was laid out very early across the marsh, and was made passable only by the corduroy laid at the bottom, remnants of which have been occasionally unearthed even of late years.

The first meeting-house was erected in 1645. It stood near the south-easterly corner of Court square, on ground now partly in the square and partly in Elm street. It was forty feet long by twenty-five wide, and fronted on the narrow lane leading to the river. There were two windows on each side and one smaller one at each end. It enjoyed the distinction of having a shingled roof instead of a thatch, and had two turrets, one designed for a bell, although not at first so occupied, and the other intended as a watch tower. One of these turrets appears to have been sometimes occupied as a school-room. At first

the meeting-house had no gallery. One was afterwards constructed when the increase of population
rendered it necessary. In this edifice the people
assembled for worship on the Sabbath, at the sound
of the drum beaten by John Matthews, up and down
the street, from the house of Mr. Moxon, the minister, which stood near the head of Vernon street,
to the house of Rowland Stebbins, something over
one hundred rods further south.

The only other public building, known to have
been here during the first forty years of our history,
was the jail or house of correction, which was not
built until after 1662. For some reason, not clearly
appearing, this was located near what is now the in-
tersection of Maple and Temple streets. In 1662 a
highway was ordered to be laid out to the house of
correction, then about to be built, and thence to the
house next to Thompson's dingle. This dingle included a large part of what is now the cemetery and
Avon place. The house referred to, I suppose to
have stood not far from the site of the house of Mr.
William Gunn. This highway was the original of the
present Maple street, although in the southerly part
of it, it diverged to the westward of the present
street, following nearly the line of the brow of the
hill. The house of correction was undoubtedly a
wooden structure of very moderate size and equip-
ment, probably sufficient for the wants of that day,
but serving only for the confinement of prisoners
awaiting trial, or under sentence for brief terms.
There was one other building erected here very
early—certainly as early as 1660—which, although a

private residence, was distinguished by some circumstances that entitle it to particular mention. This was the dwelling-house of John Pynchon, the son of William, who succeeded to all his father's honors and influence here, and bore a conspicuous part in the affairs of Western Massachusetts, until the close of the seventeenth century. This house stood on the westerly side of Main street, a little north of Fort street. The main part of it was built of brick, in a style of architecture quite peculiar. It was probably the only brick building here during that century. This house remained in the Pynchon family, and was occupied as a dwelling, until it was taken down in 1831, to make way for a more modern structure. A few of our inhabitants remember this house, which was sometimes called "the old fort," from its having been a fortified house and place of refuge during the eventful scenes of two hundred years ago. The year after it was demolished, a sketch of it from memory was drawn by the late Rev. Dr. Peabody. I have a photograph of this sketch. It is rudely represented in our city seal, and probably many other representations of it are in existence.

No event of any great local importance occurred here during the first fourteen or fifteen years after the settlement of the town. That period was one of growth—not rapid, but still of growth. Many new settlers came here during that time, and the town in a measure acquired a stability that seemed to ensure the success of the original undertaking of Pynchon and his associates. But about the year 1651, Mr. Pynchon fell under the displeasure of the General

3

Court at Boston on account of a book received there
from England, where it had been printed, which
purported to have been written by him. It was a
theological work, but its theology was not quite in
accordance with the prevailing sentiment of the
authorities at Boston, and proceedings were at once
instituted against Pynchon, in order to compel him
to retract the heresies he had advanced in this work,
or suffer the consequences of persistence in them.
He consented to modify and explain some of the
obnoxious sentiments, but not enough to meet the
demands of the General Court. The breach became
so wide that his further continuance in the colony
became very disagreeable, if not dangerous. He
was displaced from the magistracy here, and his
son-in-law, Henry Smith, appointed in his place.
It does not appear from the record, that Smith ac-
cepted the office thus conferred upon him, or performed any of its duties. Pynchon determined to return to England, and Smith chose to accompany him.
Both of them sailed for that country in 1652, and
neither ever returned to America. Mr. Moxon, the
minister, either accompanied them, or followed them
the same year. His departure was owing to some
peculiar domestic troubles that he experienced. As
early as 1649, suspicions of witchcraft began to be
entertained here, and in 1651 one Mary Parsons, the
wife of Hugh Parsons, was charged with having be-
witched the minister's two daughters, and was tried
at Boston upon this charge. The evidence of her
guilt was not satisfactory, and she was acquitted.
Mr. Moxon, either from dissatisfaction at this result,

or else from a desire to remedy the real or imagined distempers with which his children were afflicted, was induced to abandon his ministry, and return with his family to England.

The loss sustained by the departure of these three, so prominent and influential inhabitants, although a very serious one, and at the time deeply felt, did not permanently check the growth and prosperity of the town. The place of William Pynchon was soon filled by his son John, with distinguished ability and success; and the loss of Mr. Moxon was fully compensated by the arrival in 1659 of Rev. Pelatiah Glover, who soon after succeeded to Mr. Moxon's pulpit, and occupied his dwelling-house. Both of these gentlemen held a high place in the esteem of their fellow-townsmen. Mr. Glover was the religious teacher of the people for more than thirty years. He is said by a cotemporary historian to have had "a brave library" and to have been a diligent student. John Pynchon, although a young man at the time of his father's departure, was a person of very superior character and abilities, and fully qualified for the responsible stations to which he was immediately called. He was at once placed at the head of a commission, with Elizur Holyoke and Samuel Chapin as his associates, with full authority to administer the government of this town. He was soon after elected lieutenant of the military company at Springfield, and so, in the absence of his brother-in-law, Henry Smith, who had been appointed captain before he left for England, became the chief military officer here, holding successively the offices of captain, major, and eventually

of colonel, and commander-in-chief of the forces in
this part of the State.

This occasion—the anniversary of an event of the
greatest local importance in the history of this place,
makes it necessary to consider somewhat in detail the
relations sustained by the founders of Springfield to
the Indians in this vicinity, and to gather up, from
such sources as are available, the memorials of a race
of savage men that, for a century and a half, have
been strangers here.   It is hard now to realize that,
on these lovely hill-sides, and in these pleasant val-
leys, now so rich in the tokens of civilization and
culture, the rude wigwams of the red men were once
seen, that in these forests they hunted, and in these
rivers they fished.   Far back in some uncertain century of the past, they found their way to this con-
tinent, and became its wild and savage masters.   Before the tide of a later civilization, they melted away
and disappeared.   They have left us no record of
whence they came, or whither they went.   But the
mementos of their existence are still to be found—
their rude domestic implements are occasionally unearthed, and the hundreds of arrow-heads that have
been gathered by the curious, all assure us that they
once were here.   The first settlers found them in the
quiet possession of the beautiful meadows on either
side of the Connecticut.   The earliest intercourse of
the natives with the new-comers, was an act of
courtesy and kindness.   As already mentioned, the
pioneers, sent up by Pynchon from the Bay to ex-
plore and ascertain the best location for the intended
settlement, built a house in the meadow on the west

side of the river, and occupied it that summer. The Indians notified them that the place they had selected, although one of great fertility of soil, was subject to inundation in time of freshets, and they abandoned it for a safer location on the east side of the river. When Mr. Pynchon himself came with his party, he entered at once into negotiations with the Indians for the purchase of a site for the new plantation. The Indians were ready to accommodate the white strangers, and to sell to them the lands they required for their settlement. On the 15th day of July, 1636, by a formal deed, Commucke and Matanchan, two of the ancient Indians of Agawam, for themselves, and as representatives of the other Indian proprietors, conveyed to William Pynchon, Henry Smith, and John Burr, a large part of the territory, now occupied by this city, and lands in this vicinity. Eleven other Indians, representing probably the entire proprietary of the lands, affixed their marks to the instrument, in token of their assent to the bargain. These marks are of various forms, according to the fancy or the custom of the signer. Wenawis, Coa, and Machetuhood signed with the figure of an arrow. Menis and Wessaj, *alias* Nepinam, made marks representing a bow and arrow. Winnepawin's mark resembles a pitcher or jar.*

The whole purport and effect of the deed was made known and explained to the signers by Ahaughton, an Indian interpreter from the bay, so that they fully understood the transaction. For this purchase, Mr. Pynchon paid the Indians " 18 fathom

---

* Appendix E.

of wampum, 18 coates, 18 hatchets, 18 howes, and 18 knives," which, by the standard of value in that day, was a very adequate price. Two extra coats were given to Wrutherna, one of the Indians, and full liberty reserved to them all to take fish and deer, groundnuts, walnuts, acorns and a kind of peas. It does not appear that the Indians ever complained that they were not fully paid for this land. On the contrary, they afterwards made other conveyances, one of them as late as 1674, in which this deed was referred to and confirmed.

It is not likely that the Indians, then inhabiting the territory, now occupied by this city, were very numerous. One writer states the number of warriors here at about forty. Upon this basis, the whole number, women and children included, was probably not far from two hundred. The lands retained by them were ample for their wants,—so ample that, from time to time, they made other sales to the agents of the town, as the increase of population made it desirable to enlarge the borders of the settlement.

The trade in beaver and other furs, in which Mr. Pynchon was extensively engaged, afforded the Indians a ready market for their peltry. To facilitate this trade, Mr. Pynchon early established a warehouse near the southern limit of what was then considered Springfield. This warehouse was at Warehouse Point, which owes its name to that circumstance. The limits of the town in that direction, by order of the General Court, passed in March, 1648, were to extend twenty rods below that warehouse.

The friendly relations, established between the settlers and the Indians, by William Pynchon and his
coadjutors, continued inviolate through the whole
period of his residence here, and for more than
twenty years afterwards. John Pynchon pursued
the same wise policy in his dealings with them that
his father had pursued. One feature of this policy
was, to treat the Indians as an independent people,
so far as not to regard them as amenable to his jurisdiction for their treatment of each other, except for
offences committed within the territory owned by
the white settlers. If one Indian wronged another
in any place outside of these limits, the matter was
left to be redressed by the Indians themselves in
their own fashion. This policy was advocated in a
letter, written by William Pynchon to Lieut.-Gover-
nor Dudley in 1648. Some Indians near Quaboag,
now Brookfield, had been murdered by some Naucotak Indians. The friends of the murdered men applied to the authorities at Boston for assistance to ar-
rest the murderers. As the Naucotaks were only about
fifteen miles distant from Springfield, Mr. Pynchon
was directed to render the necessary aid in bringing
the murderers to justice. In his answer to Lieut.-
Governor Dudley, he set forth so clearly the want of
jurisdiction over the Indians under such circumstances, that the attempt to interfere was at once
. abandoned.* But in regard to offences committed
by the Indians against our own people, both the
Pynchons frequently exercised their jurisdiction, and
awarded to the offenders such punishment as a wise

* Appendix F.

and just policy dictated, at the same time carefully
avoiding any appearance of unnecessary harshness.
It was intended that the administration of justice
should commend itself to the Indians, as in itself
reasonable and proper. So, when the house of
Rowland Thomas was broken open by an Indian
thief, and the good wife's wardrobe plundered, William Pynchon issued his warrant to the constable to
search for the thief and the stolen property. This
warrant, as recorded in his private book of records,
is a curious document in itself, and at the same time
illustrates Pynchon's method of dealing with the
Indians.   It is in these words :

"To Tho. Merrick, *Constable of Springfield:*

"By virtue hereof, you are to make inquiry among our Indians on the other side" (meaning the west side of the river),
"what Indian hath broken open Rowland's house, and taken away
her best new kersey petticote & some linin in a Baskett, &˙you are
to bring the Indian before me, or the goode, if he make an escape, that they may be delivered to the owner.

W. Pynchon.
Springfield 20 July 1650."

Then follows this supplementary document :

"If you find him at Woronoco " (Westfield) "you may persuade
him to come, and push him forward to make him come, but in
case you cannot make him come by this means, then you shall
not use violence, but rather leave him.

William Pynchon.
Springfield, the day aforesaid."

It turned out that the thief was not one of " our
Indians," but an Indian from near New Haven by the
name of Munnackquass, and that, although he was
arrested at Woronoco by the constable, he succeeded
in making his escape, through the connivance of the

Woronoco Indians. Three days afterwards, Attum-
bahad, the sachem at Woronoco, with some other
Indians, called at Mr. Pynchon's house, to excuse himself from blame in this transaction, by charging some
stranger Indians with aiding the escape of the prisoner. Mr. Pynchon answered the sachem, that the
English came to him as friends, and desired him to
let them have the prisoner in a friendly way, and
after they had captured him and bound him, and left
him temporarily in the hands of this Woronoco
sachem for safe keeping, he had allowed other Indians
to rescue him, without making any resistance or giving any alarm, and so was to be accounted as one
with the guilty person. This logic was too much for
the sachem to answer, and he proposed to com-
promise by paying three fathoms of wampum. Mr.
Pynchon declined this as too little, but offered to
accept five fathoms and the petticoat, and the difficulty was settled upon those terms, and Goody
Thomas had her garment again.

Justice sometimes overtook the Indian culprit, after
a long delay, in an unexpected manner. Thus, an
Indian, who lived somewhere above Hadley, had been
guilty of breaking the windows of Mr. Pynchon's
farm-house, and other "miscarriages." Some years
elapsed, and, either because the offender was un-
known, or because he kept out of the way, he had
escaped the penalty. But unwisely, as it turned out,
he had run in debt to John Scott, and, in 1655,
Scott, chancing to fall in with him, had him before
John Pynchon and Elizur Holyoke, who were then
commissioners to hold courts at Springfield, for the

4

purpose of collecting his debt. Wattawhunksin, (for
that was his name,) had not only to pay his debt to
John Scott, but, being recognized as the person, who
years before had committed the trespasses upon
Mr. Pynchon's farm-house, was also obliged to give
security for the payment of that damage.

In the cases already mentioned, the offenders appear to have been Indians from other places. But it
was not always so. One Sunday forenoon in May,
1671, when "Sam. Bliss" and his wife were at meeting, an Indian by the name of Aquossowump, who
had been loitering about Bliss's premises the previous
week, came to his house, and, finding only children
at home, went to a chest, in which Mrs. Bliss had
some wampum, and, although the children got upon
the top of the chest to keep the lid down, yet, being
stronger than they, he opened it and took out the
wampum. Upon being arrested and examined, he
was fully identified by the children and admitted the
offence, although, like many other rogues, he endeavored to extenuate it. But, as the Pynchon record reads, "his theft was evident and on the Sabbath
also, & going into the house, stealing as is thought
above 20 fathum of wampum, 1 ordered him to pay
his spare coate & y° wampum found with him
(all which was delivered Sam. Bliss), and also sen-
tenced him to be well whipped with 20 lashes, which
was executed by y° constable." Wampum was by law
recognized as money in transactions with the Indians,
and was frequently the subject of their larcenies.

There were occasionally difficulties between the
Indians and the whites, but these were usually of

a trifling character. Nor were the Indians always the aggressors. There were some troublesome men among the whites. Thomas Miller, of whom more will be said in the sequel, appears to have been one of this character. (In 1650 the sons of Reippumsink, who was probably one of the older Indians, complained to the elder Pynchon, that Miller, then a young man, had committed an assault upon their father, by striking him with the butt of his gun. It was a serious charge, and a due regard to impartial justice between his own fellow-citizen and his Indian neighbors, required the gravest consideration. Mr. Pynchon therefore gave dignity to the occasion by calling to his assistance Mr. Moxon, the reverend minister of the town, Thomas Merrick, George Colton, and Thomas Cooper, highly respectable citizens, together with his own son, John Pynchon. By their advice, it was ordered that Miller should be whipped fifteen lashes, as a punishment for the assault. But, before this sentence was executed, Thomas Miller made his peace with the Indians, by paying them four fathoms of wampum. Ten years later, in 1660, Miller was involved in another difficulty with some Nipmuck Indians, which brought him again before the local court as a complainant. The story is thus told in the Pynchon record:

"May 9, 1660. Thomas Miller complayned ag^t certayne Indians y^t came to his house, wch, as his wife sayth, scarred his children by throwinge stickes at them: his wife cominge out of her house & callinge to her husband for help, he was going into his house to fetch a cudgell & his wife followed him & at the doore of his house one of the Indians stroke his wife on her head with his fist y^t shee fell down with the blow: & Thomas Miller

turninge back layd hold on the Indian that struck his wife:
then another of the Indians laid hold on Tho. Miller & rescued
him y' struck y° woman & the other Indians struck Tho. Miller
diverse blows while he & the Indian were scuffling: the Indians being pursued by diverse men & horses, three of them
were taken & brought before y° three commissioners, two of
which Indians were found guilty in y° case but the Indian that
stroke the woman could not be taken: the names of those y'
were taken & found guilty were Kollabauggamitt & Maullamaug
who dwell in Nipmuck country they were adjudged to pay for
themselves & y° rest y' escaped 14 fathom of wampum: the Indians paying the wampum 6 fathom was delivered to y° constable
to defray the charges of 10 men & 5 horses that pursued them
or y' were required to waite on the service & 8 fathoms was
given to Tho. Miller in way of satisfaction for y° injury done to
him & his wife."

Thomas Miller was unquestionably a brave, stout
man, and evidently bore no special good will toward
the Indians, being ever ready, when occasion offered,
to engage in a fray with them.   It is to be observed,
however, that these Indians were not "our" Indians,
but Nipmucks, a tribe inhabiting the southern part
of Worcester county, and the adjacent portions of
Connecticut.

So far as the Springfield Indians were concerned,
they appear to have conducted themselves as orderly
and peaceably, as did the white inhabitants.   Occasional breaches of law occurred among our own people,
and so far as appears, they were no more frequent
among the Indians, inhabiting this town and the vicinity.   The most amicable relations existed between
them and the people of the town.   They visited their
houses freely, and bartered their wares; they strolled
up and down our Main street, conversing in their bro-

ken way with their English acquaintance, and their canoes floated in our river. As much confidence was mutually felt, as could be expected between people, differing so widely in their habits, and modes of life, and thought. The disorders that occurred were as rare as in any community of later times, and were produced by essentially similar causes. They were not at all owing to any prejudice or antipathy of race.

In all these relations with their Indian neighbors, the people of Springfield appear to have been more fortunate than many of the early settlers in other towns.

Until the year 1675, nothing occurred to disturb this harmony. In that year commenced that famous Indian outbreak, known as King Philip's war.

Philip was the second son of the celebrated Massasoit, sachem of the Wampanoags, long the friend of the whites. After the death of his older brother Alexander, Philip succeeded to the chieftaincy of his tribe, and soon became embroiled in difficulties with the English. He endeavored to unite all the principal tribes of New England in one grand confederacy against the colonists, in the hope either to expel or exterminate them. His first effort was to secure the co-operation of the Narragansett Indians, a powerful tribe, occupying the region about the western shore of the Narragansett Bay. Failing at first to secure their aid, Philip soon found himself so hard pressed by the English and their allies, the Mohegan Indians, that he was forced to retire from Bristol county, and the adjacent parts of Rhode Island where his tribe was chiefly located, into

the interior of this State among the Nipmuck Indians.
These joined him in his raids upon the towns in Worcester county, and those upon the Connecticut river.   One
of the towns that suffered early and most severely was
Quaboag, now Brookfield, which was attacked in August, 1675.   After drawing Captain Hutchinson and
Captain Wheeler, who had been sent with a party of
soldiers to negotiate a treaty with them, into an ambush
at a swamp about ten miles from the town, the Indians
suddenly attacked them, killed eight of the men, mortally wounded Captain Hutchinson and two others, and
pursued the survivors to the village.   There the soldiers and all the inhabitants, about eighty in all, including women and children, hastily took refuge in one
house.   The Indians burned all the other houses,
twenty or more in number, and for three or four days,
besieged this house, making all the while, persistent
but ineffectual attempts to set it on fire.   At last the
garrison were relieved by the arrival of Major Wil-
lard, with fifty mounted men.   Soon after this, Philip's
Indians made their appearance on the Connecticut
river at Deerfield, where they burned a number of
houses.   The next day, they attacked Northfield, and
killed several men.   On the third of September, Captain Richard Beers of Watertown, on his way with
thirty-six men to reinforce the garrison at Northfield, was attacked by Indians, and twenty of the
men, with Captain Beers himself, were killed.

A few days later, on the eighteenth of September,
occurred the famous massacre at Bloody Brook, where
Captain Thomas Lathrop of Beverly, and eighty-eight
young men, "the flower of Essex," were surprised by

a superior force of Indians, and seventy of their number slaughtered.

Philip himself is supposed to have commanded the
Indians in both these fights, but this is not certainly
known.

These assaults of Philip upon the upper towns on our
river were attended with the barbarities that have
usually characterized Indian warfare, and excited general attention and sympathy. The colonial authorities
of Massachusetts and Connecticut, were aroused to the
importance of vigorous measures against the common
enemy, and both sent their forces to protect the en-
dangered towns. Those of Massachusetts were under
Major John Pynchon, as commander-in-chief. Those
of Connecticut were commanded by Major Treat of
Hartford. Among the subordinate Massachusetts
officers, who took an active part in the campaign, were
Captain Samuel Appleton, and Captain Moseley.

The policy of the colonial authorities at Boston, at
this period of the war, was, not to maintain regular
garrisons in the frontier towns for their protection, but
to dispatch military forces in pursuit of the enemy,
wherever they appeared. But in this kind of strategy
the Indians were much greater adepts than the English.
They were perfectly familiar with all the paths, by
which the forests could be traversed. Their move-
ments were stealthy and rapid. They fell upon the
amazed and bewildered settlements, when least expected, executed their savage and bloody work with
fearful rapidity, and then disappeared as suddenly as
they had come, leaving little or no trace of their
course. It was to little purpose that, when tidings

reached the nearest military force, detachments were
sent in pursuit. Generally they reached the scene,
only to find the smoking ruins of houses, that the
savages had burned, and the mutilated and ghastly remains of those who had been their occupants.

Major Pynchon had become satisfied of the impolicy
of this course, and had advised the commissioners,
who had the direction of the campaign, that the true
course to be pursued, was, to place garrisons in all the
exposed towns, sufficient to protect them in case of an
attack. This had been done in some of the towns,
but the commissioners had not yet seen fit to adopt
this policy generally. In case of an alarm in quarters
not adequately protected, the garrison soldiers were
required to march to their relief.

In this way it happened that Major Pynchon, with
all the force under his command at Springfield, about
forty-five in number, was summoned to march northward on the 4th of October, 1675, O. S., (answering
to October 15th of the present calendar,) by tidings
that a considerable body of Indians had been discovered,
about five or six miles from Hadley. To attack this
enemy, the English forces were ordered to concentrate
in that town. So that, when the night of October
4th closed in upon the inhabitants of Springfield, they
were entirely without military defence. Their own
militia were with Major Pynchon at Hadley, or on
their march toward that place. Major Treat, with
his Connecticut forces, was on the west side of the
river at a considerable distance from this town.

Notwithstanding the defenceless condition of Springfield, and the tendency of current events to awaken

anxiety, its inhabitants seem to have felt no serious apprehension of danger threatening this town. Why should they ? Philip and his warriors were understood to be engaged in operations against the towns up the river, where he had the sympathy and co-operation of the Indians of that vicinity.

The Springfield Indians were their own neighbors, with whom for nearly forty years, they had lived in daily and friendly intercourse. These were not supposed to have entered into any confederacy with Philip. They professed their steadfast friendship for our people. To allay any uneasiness that might exist, and emphasize their assurances of fidelity, they had even given hostages, who were sent to Hartford for greater security.

Whatever anxieties the disturbances north of them may at first have occasioned, the people here felt that, so long as the Springfield Indians were true to them, Philip could do them no harm.

Such was the feeling of security, with which the inhabitants of this town retired to their rest on the evening of Monday, the 4th of October, 1675. Their sympathies were warmly enlisted for the settlers in other towns, less favorably situated, to whose relief their husbands, and brothers, and sons had gone, and they doubtless offered fervent prayers that they might be preserved from the dangers that threatened them. For themselves and their families here, they felt safe, and so they laid themselves down on that memorable Monday night to a quiet sleep.

While such was the feeling of composure here, twenty miles down the river at Windsor, there was one person,

5

whose bosom was agitated with emotions so powerful,
that they could not be concealed. This person was an
Indian, named Toto, who was domesticated in the
family of Mr. Wolcott, and was friendly to the English.
He was in possession of a secret, that stirred the very
depths of his nature. Upon being questioned by the
family, and urged to explain the cause of his manifest
distress, he at length revealed the fact, which had in
some way become known to him, that a plot had been
formed to destroy Springfield, and that, for this purpose, a large body of Philip's men had been treacherously admitted by the Springfield Indians to their fort.
This fort was situated on Long Hill, about a mile south
from the central part of the town. The precise location is supposed to have been at the head of a ravine,
running down from the brow of the hill, west of the
present Long Hill street, toward the Connecticut
river.

Upon the disclosure of this plot by Toto, immediately
a swift messenger was dispatched to warn the people
here of their danger, and another sent to Major Treat
with similar information. The messenger arrived here
in the night. The alarm was immediately given to all
the inhabitants, and a messenger sent to Major Pynchon
at Hadley for help.

At that time there were three fortified houses here.
One was the brick house of Major Pynchon, already
noticed, standing near the head of Fort street. Two
others were near the southerly end of Main street, the
lower one perhaps not far from Broad street.

Roused at midnight from their slumbers by notice
of the impending danger, the villagers fled at once to

these fortified houses, taking with them in their flight such of their more valuable effects as they could readily remove. Every preparation was made for defence that the nature of the case would admit of. But there was a painful consciousness that, if an immediate assault was made by the Indians, the issue would be doubtful. There were some brave men and heroic women within the forts. Some of the leading men of the town were there. Deacon Samuel Chapin, one of the associates of Major Pynchon in the magistracy, and ancestor of all of that name in this country, was one of this number. Jonathan Burt, for a time the town clerk, was another. There too was Thomas Cooper, the lieutenant of the military company, who had, but a short time before, led a party of soldiers, that marched from Springfield to the relief of burning Brookfield. These were wise and courageous men, but they were considerably advanced in life. The young and able-bodied men, who composed the military force of the town, were mostly absent with Major Pynchon at Hadley. Elizur Holyoke, the captain of the company, although not a young man, was probably with his command, and his son, Samuel Holyoke, who distinguished himself so much the next year in the famous fight at Turner's Falls, undoubtedly was with the troops at Hadley. More than all, the people at Springfield felt the absence of Major Pynchon himself, who, beyond any other man, possessed their confidence. Under these circumstances, the people in the fortified houses watched with sleepless anxiety for any indication of an enemy.

The night wore away, and the morning of Tuesday,

October 5th, dawned upon the watchers. It brought no
confirmation of their fears; the risen sun disclosed no
savage foes. The houses, stretched along the street,
showed no signs of having been molested. Everything remained so quiet, that the impression prevailed
in many minds that the alarm was a false one. The
Rev. Mr. Glover, the minister, was so certain that
there was no real danger to be apprehended, that he
removed back to his own house his library, which had
been transferred for safety to Major Pynchon's house.
This opinion of one so much respected, doubtless tended
much to shake the faith of others in the reality of the
danger. Of the number that questioned the truth of
the report from Windsor, was Lieutenant Cooper, who
determined to test its accuracy by a personal visit to
the Indian fort. Taking with him Thomas Miller, the
two set out on horseback down the Main Street toward
Long Hill. They had passed about a quarter of a
mile beyond the most southerly house, and entered
the woods, which then skirted the settlement in that
direction, but had not crossed Mill river, when their
further progress was suddenly arrested by a discharge
of fire-arms from some unseen foes. Miller was in-
stantly killed. Cooper was fatally shot, and fell from
his horse, but being an athletic and resolute man, he
contrived to mount again, and turned and rode at full
speed back to the nearest fort. Before reaching it
he received a second shot from the savages, who were
in full pursuit, and died as he reached the fort.

The Indians then burst upon the town with the
greatest fury.

"* * * Alas, that direful yell,
So loud, so wild, so shrill, so clear,
As if the very fiends of hell,
Burst from the wildwood depths, were here."

Unable to gratify their thirst for blood, by the slaughter of the people within the forts, they began the work of destroying their undefended houses, barns, and other property. The whole number of dwelling-houses in the town was forty-five, and in a short time thirty-two of these dwellings and twenty-four or twenty-five barns were in flames.

The house of correction was destroyed.

Major Pynchon's corn-mill and saw-mill were burned, and in general the corn and hay, in store for the coming winter, were consumed.

Besides Cooper and Miller, one woman, Pentecost Matthews, wife of John Matthews, the drummer, who lived near the South end of the street, was killed. Four other persons were wounded, one of them, Edmund Pringrydays, so severely that he died a few days afterwards.

From one end of the street to the other, this scene of havoc and devastation was exhibited. The beleaguered people looked out guardedly from the windows and loop-holes of the fortified houses, and saw the Indians, whom they had known familiarly as neighbors and friends for years—to whom they had done no wrong—ruthlessly apply the torch to their dwellings, and consign them, with their furniture, their stores of food, and all those little provisions they had made for the comfort of their families during the approaching winter, to a remorseless destruction.

In this diabolical work the Springfield Indians, some forty in number, were not a whit behind the strangers, whom they had admitted to their fort. Indeed, first and foremost in this work, " the ringleader in word and deed," as Rev. John Russell, of Hadley, wrote the next day to Governor Leverett, was Wequogan, the· chief sachem of the Springfield Indians, " a man in whom as much confidence had been placed by the settlers as in any of the Indians.*" Another chief, well known to our people, while actively engaged in this mischief loudly proclaimed to them that he was one who had burned Quabog, and would serve them the same way.

The assailants did not go entirely unscathed in this work of destruction. Some of them were shot from the fortified houses. It is said that one of them, who had taken a large pewter platter from one of the deserted houses, received a mortal wound by a bullet through the platter, which he was vainly using as a shield. Hoyt, in his " History of the Indian Wars," states that at the time he wrote, this platter, with a bullet-hole through it, was still preserved in Springfield, as a memento of that day. Where is that relic now ?

While these scenes were being enacted in our street, it was ascertained, at about eleven or twelve o'clock, that Major Treat, with his Connecticut troops, had arrived on the west bank of the river opposite the town. The commonly received account is that he had marched from Westfield. This may be true. But the letter of Mr. Russell, written the next day, leads to

* Appendix G.

the inference that his line of march was from the
north, rather than the west. There were no boats on
the west side of the river, so that Major Treat had
no means of crossing. But his arrival being perceived
by our men on this side, five of them attempted to
reach him with a boat. Twenty Indians pursued them
as they left the garrison, but they succeeded in taking
one boat across, which was speedily filled with soldiers,
and started for the Eastern shore. But it was soon
found impossible to effect a landing. The Indians, assembled on the high bank, were able to pour a deadly
fire into the boat as it approached, without being themselves exposed to a return fire, and so the attempt to
relieve the burning town in this way had to be for the
time abandoned. The savages still had everything
their own way outside of the forts, and the demon of
destruction reigned unchecked for some hours longer.
Nearly all historians of the events of that day have
assigned to Major Treat the credit of relieving the
burning town. But not to him does it belong. All
honor to Major Treat and the gallant men of Connecticut for what they endeavored to do. They failed
of success from causes beyond their control, and the
rescue was delayed.

All this while, two hundred armed men, including
the Springfield soldiers, were marching from Hadley
toward this town, under the command of Major
Pynchon, with all the resolution and earnestness that
could be inspired by a sense of the danger that
threatened the town and its unprotected inhabitants,
and a desire to preserve their homes from the flames,
and their families and friends from the terrible cruelties

of Indian warfare. "It was a march," says Captain Appleton, the second in command, "that put all our men into a most violent sweat, and was more than they could well bear." On they came, with an energy that never slacked. How anxiously must they have watched the southern horizon, to discover, if possible, if there were any signs of trouble at Springfield. And when, as they rose some height, that enlarged their field of vision, and saw the cloud of smoke rising in the distance, and hovering over the devoted town, what various and conflicting emotions must have rushed upon them, quickening them to exertions well-nigh desperate.

At two or three o'clock in the afternoon. they reached the town, and the whole scene of desolation was before them. The flames were still rising from the ruins of fifty-seven buildings, thirty-two of them houses, and twenty-five barns. From the north end of the street, until they came to Major Pynchon's, not a house or barn was standing, except the house of an old man by the name of William Branch; between Pynchon's house and the meeting-house, the house of Rev. Mr. Glover, John Hitchcock, John Stewart, and several others were burned with their barns. A few houses were standing about the meeting-house, or the present Elm street. From the house of Thomas Merrick, a little below where West State street now is, down to the two garrison houses at the lower end of Main street, all were destroyed. In one of those garrison houses lay the body of the brave Lieutenant Thomas Cooper, killed in the morning. He was a man between fifty and sixty years of age, and had been a

resident of the town more than thirty years. He was
a carpenter by trade, and in 1645 built the first
meeting-house. In 1668 he was chosen a deputy to
the General Court. He appears also to have had considerable skill and practice as a bone-setter, being often
called upon to go from place to place in the old
county of Hampshire for that purpose, there being
then probably no regular surgeon in the county.
This service he had performed without compensation.
His usefulness in this capacity was expressly recognized by the County Court in March, 1675, and
measures adopted to secure him a suitable compensation. But, before any further action was taken by
the court, Lieutenant Cooper was killed.

The Indians were aware of the approach of Major
Pynchon and his troops, and although they had been
able to baffle the attempts of Major Treat to relieve
the town, they now found themselves obliged to with-
draw. And so, when Pynchon and his men reached
the burning town, the savages had all disappeared.

It is easier to conceive than to describe, with what
mingled emotions of joy and sorrow Major Pynchon
and his suffering townsmen met. The people wel-
comed his return as their leader and counselor; one
in whose wisdom they could confide, to guide and
help them in their deep distress. On the other hand,
Pynchon felt overwhelmed with the sudden and terrible calamity that had fallen upon the town, whose
affairs he had so largely directed for nearly a quarter
of a century, and with all whose interests his own
were so closely identified. He, as well as his neighbors, was personally a great loser. His mills and barns

6

were consumed. And how should the people be supplied with bread during the coming winter, now that the crops, just gathered, were all destroyed ?

On the very day that he reached this town, and saw the devastation that had been wrought by the Indians, he wrote a letter to his friend from whom he had just parted, the Rev. John Russell, of Hadley, announcing the disaster in these words:

Springfeild Octo. 5. 75

Reverend S^r

  The Ld will haue vs ly in ye dust before him: we y^t were full are emptyed. But it is ye Ld & blessed be his holy name: we came to a Lamentable & woefull sight The Towne in flames not a house nor Barne standing except old Goodm Branches till we came to my house & then Mr Glovers John Hitchcocks & Goodm Stewart burnt downe wth Barnes Corne & all they had: a few standing about ye Meeting house & then from Miricks downward all burnt to 2 Garrison houses at ye Lower end of ye Towne my Grist Mill & Corne Mill Burnt downe: wth some other houses & Barns I had let out to Tenants: All Mr Glovers library Burnt wth all his Corne so y^t he hath none to live on as well as myselfe & Many more: y^t haue not for subsistence they tell me 32 houses & ye Barns belonging to y^m are Burnt & all ye Livelyhood of ye owners, & what more may meete wth ye same stroaks ye Ld only knows

  many more had there estats Burnt in these houses: so y^t I beleeue 40 famylys are vtterly destitute of Subsistence ye Ld shew mercy to vs I se not how it is Posible for vs to live here this winter & If so the sooner we were holpen off ye Better:

  S^r I Pray acqvaint o^r Honord Govr wth this dispensation of God I know not how to write neither can I be able to attend any Publike service   the L^d in mercy speake to my heart & to all o^r hearts is ye Reall desire of   Yo^{rs} to serve yo^u

JOHN PYNCHON

I Pray send downe by ye Post my doblet: Cote Linnen &c I left there & Papers &c

This letter was forwarded by Mr. Russell to Governor Leverett, together with one of his own.* Three days later, on the 8th of October, Major Pynchon made an official report to the Governor.† From these cotemporary documents, and the correspondence of Major Appleton,‡ many of the facts, connected with the burning of the town, have been gathered. They furnish the most reliable statement of the events of that day.

One of the first measures, adopted after the arrival of the troops, was the sending out scouts to ascertain in what direction the enemy had retired, that they might be pursued and punished. But every effort to do this proved fruitless. The trails found indicated various lines of retreat. At first it was thought they had gone south. Then a later discovery pointed toward a route northward. On the 8th of October, when Major Pynchon prepared his official report, the direction taken by the Indians had not been satisfactorily ascertained. An old squaw, who was captured here a few days after the attack, stated that the Indians made their first halt about six miles away, and at that point remains of twenty-four fires and some plunder were found. This is said to have been in the vicinity of Indian Orchard, or Jenksville.

Of the number of Indians, engaged in this attack on the town, there is nothing certainly known. The commonly received statement is that there were three hundred of Philip's men, besides the Springfield Indians. These latter are stated by a cotemporary anonymous author to have been about forty in num-

---

* Appendix II. † Appendix I. ‡ Appendix K.

ber. He imputes the whole mischief to them, and says nothing about any accession of Philip's men.

This author, who styles himself "a merchant of Boston," and addresses his communication to a friend in London, calls these Indians " Praying Indians," a term applied not only to those converted under the ministry of the celebrated missionary, John Elliot, but also to other small communities of red men, who were partially civilized, and lived near and in constant intercourse with the whites. To this latter class the Springfield Indians may properly be assigned. There is no evidence that there were any Christianized Indians among them.

The testimony, derived from parties who were here at the time, varies largely as to the number. The message sent by post to Major Pynchon at Hadley, was, that there were five hundred Indians about to attack the town. The estimate, communicated to Mr. Russell, of Hadley, the next day from those who were in the fortified houses, was that there appeared not above one hundred Indians in all. But then it must have been difficult for the men shut up in these forts to determine with any accuracy the number of the whooping incendiaries, who were flitting from house to house, and barn to barn, applying their torches, and raising yells of triumph as the flames ascended. The Indians did not parade in line to be counted, and if they had, the men inside the forts would have used the opportunity for some other purpose than counting them. Perhaps the statement made by the squaw who was captured, furnishes as reliable an estimate as any in regard to the number of the assailants. She said the number of Indians who came to Springfield was two hundred and seventy, and was a part of their whole force of six hundred, whose rendezvous was at a place called Coassett, supposed to be about fifty miles above Hadley.

It is difficult for us to appreciate the effect of this disaster upon the people, to whom this town had been till then a home. It was most depressing. A feeling of despondency, amounting almost to despair, settled down upon the minds of a majority of the inhabitants. They had seen the town, which some of them had aided to plant—which most of them had helped to nurture—whose growth, slow but steady, they had watched and rejoiced in from year to year, in a single day, within a few hours, reduced to ruin. Two-thirds of its homes, which industry and enterprise had reared, where happy families had dwelt, were now heaps of ashes. The barns into which the crops of the year, the fruits of their summer's toil, had been garnered, had been swept away, with their contents, as by the besom of destruction. If any were so fortunate as to save their Indian corn or other grain, they had no mills where it could be ground and prepared for use. The winter was coming on, and they knew by experience the severity of New England winters. Without houses to shelter them, without food for themselves and their cattle, removed a long distance from all sources of relief for their present wants, or supply for their future needs, is it to be wondered at that these settlers on the Connecticut were discouraged, and ready to say that they must abandon this outpost of civilized life, and seek a

home where they should be nearer to friends and
help?

Not only were they without houses and barns, and
food, and any present means of supplying this want,
but there was also the sense of insecurity, that, perhaps, more than any other cause, led them to consider the question, whether they should abandon
Springfield. For nearly forty years they had enjoyed
the blessings of peace. Although the Indians were
in their immediate vicinity, and in habits of familiar
intercourse with them, seen daily in their street,
visiting their houses, known to them almost as well
as their white neighbors, yet all this time, no trouble
had arisen between them, to cause serious apprehension of danger.

Now these friendly relations had been rudely and
suddenly shattered. The most solemn pledges of
amity had been treacherously violated by the Indians,
who had seized the opportunity, when their soldiers
were absent, to destroy the town, with the purpose to
massacre its inhabitants. A part of this design had
been accomplished. Three brave men and one unof-
fending woman had been slain, and others wounded,
and the incendiary torch applied to more than fifty
buildings. Nothing but the interposition of an overruling Providence, that gave them warning of the
danger, in time to flee to their garrison houses, saved
the people from a ruthless massacre.

Now although their foes had retired, on the approach of the military force, yet where might they
not then be lurking, ready to renew the work of fire
and blood the first moment that occasion should offer?

They had identified themselves with the cause of
Philip, and under the lead of that wily and able chief,
they might be expected to renew their attempt to
exterminate this settlement.

So the people were disheartened, and ready to remove
to some safer place. The best men of the town probably sympathized with this feeling. Rev. Mr. Glover,
the revered minister of this people, then in the full
vigor of middle life, had been a severe sufferer in this
calamity, and the ties that bound him to Springfield
had been weakened. His house had been burned, and
with it his very valuable library, of which he had
been very fond. Not even a Bible was left him. The
meeting-house, in which he had met his people from
Sabbath to Sabbath, had indeed escaped the fire, but
it had become old and inadequate to the wants of the
town, and a new structure had been decided upon
before the Indian outbreak. Sensible of the weakened state of his flock, the pastor would not, under
these circumstances, be likely to exert his influence
against the project of abandoning the town.

Major Pynchon shared in the first feeling of despondency. Indeed it came upon him with the pres-
sure of added responsibility, which the disaster cast
upon him. Owing to peculiar circumstances of affliction, he had previously expressed his earnest desire
to the Council at Boston, to be relieved from the
further command of the military forces on the Connecticut River, and the Council, on the very day pre-
ceding the destruction of the town, had yielded to his
request, and had conferred the command upon Captain
Appleton. This, of course, did not reach Pynchon

until after the affair was over, but when it came it
afforded him sensible relief, and enabled him to de-
vote himself more entirely to the work of providing
for the comfort of his fellow townsmen, and the re-
building of the town.

When the first shock of the disaster was over, a
better feeling came gradually to prevail. A deep
sense of the importance of maintaining the settlement,
so auspiciously begun, so long and carefully cherished,
and a conviction of the impolicy of surrendering the
ground to their enemies, and of the danger to other
frontier towns, that would result from an abandon-
ment of this, soon pervaded the minds of the people,
and determined the best and truest men here to hold
on. Added to all this, there was, on the part of the
leading men of Springfield, an abiding faith in an
overruling Providence, who would protect and bless
them in the way of duty. They rallied around
Major Pynchon, and gave and received a new inspira-
tion of confidence and courage.

The Colonial government too adopted beneficent
measures in behalf of the suffering town, lessening
its burdens of taxation, and making a liberal allowance for expenses incurred.

A kind Providence favored the people. The following winter, from which so much distress had been
anticipated, proved to be one of rare mildness. A re-
markably fruitful season followed. The town was rapidly rebuilt, and although for a time occasional acts of
violence, perpetrated in the neighborhood, indicated
that straggling parties of Indians lurked at no great
distance, there was no further attack upon the town.

The vigorous action of the united colonies of Massachusetts, Plymouth, and Connecticut against their common foe, resulted in the complete route of Philip's forces, and the death of the great sachem himself. Peace again returned to shed its benign influence upon the people of New England. This town shared in its blessings, and, under its favor, has maintained its onward course through all the vicissitudes of the centuries that have followed, until the little hamlet of 1675 has become the thronged and busy city of to-day. And we, as we look back to the events of that day, whose anniversary we now commemorate, and recall the changes that two centuries have wrought in the two races of men that were the actors and the sufferers of that fatal day, can appreciate the sentiment expressed by one of New England's gifted poets:

"Two hundred years! two hundred years,
    How much of human power and pride,
What glorious hopes, what gloomy fears
    Have sunk beneath their noiseless tide!

The red man at his horrid rite,
    Seen by the stars at night's cold noon,
His bark canoe, its track of light
    Left on the wave beneath the moon;

His dance, his yell, his council-fire,
    The altar where his victim lay,
His death-song, and his funeral pyre,
    That still, strong tide hath borne away.

And that pale pilgrim band is gone,
    That on this shore with trembling trod,
Ready to faint, yet bearing on
    The ark of freedom and of God.
7

Chief, sachem, sage, bards, heroes, seers,
  That live in story and in song,
Time, for the last two hundred years,
  Has raised, and shown, and swept along.

'Tis like a dream when one awakes,
  This vision of the scenes of old;
'Tis like the moon when morning breaks,
  'Tis like a tale round watch-fires told."

APPENDIX.

———•••———

A.

"May the 14th, 1636. We, whose names are underwritten, being by God's Providence, ingaged together to make a plantation, at and over against *Agaam* on Conecticot doe mutually agree to certayne articles and orders to be observed and kept by us and by our successors, except wee and every of us, for ourselves and in oure persons, shall think meet uppon better reasons to alter our present resolutions.

"1ly. Wee intend, by God's grace, as soon as we can, with all convenient speede, to procure some Godly and faithfull minister, with whome we purpose to joyne in church covenant, to walk in all the ways of Christ.

"2ly. Wee intend, that our towne, shall be composed of fourty familys, or if wee think meete after, to alter our purpose; yet not to exceed the number of fifty familys rich and poore.

"3ly. That every inhabitant shall have a convenient proportion for a house lott, as we shall see meete for every ones quality and estate.

"4ly. That every one, that hath a house lott shall have a proportion of the Cow pasture to the north of End brook, lying northward from the town; and also that every one shall have a share, of the *hassoky marish* over agaynst his lott, if it be to be had, and every one to have his proportionable share of all the woodland.

"5ly. That every one, shall have a share, of the meddow, or planting ground, over against them as nigh as may be, on Agaam side.

"6ly. That the Longmeddowe, called Masacksick, lying in the way to *Dorchester** shall be distributed to every man, as wee shall think meete, except we shall find other conveniences, for some for theyre milch cattayle and other cattayle also.

———
* Windsor, then called Dorchester.

"7ly. That the meddowe and pasture called, *Nayas* towards Patuckett, on ye side of Agaam, lyeinge about fower miles above in the ridge shall be distributed" [erasure of six and a half lines,] "as above said in the former order, and this was altered and with consent before the hands were set to it.

"8ly. That all rates that shall arise upon the town, shall be layed upon lands, according to every ones proportion, aker for aker, of howse lotts, and aker for aker of meddowe, both alike on this side, and both alike on the other side; and for farmes, that shall lye farther off, a less proportion, as wee shall after agree except wee shall see meete to remitt one half of the rate from land to other estate.

"9ly. That whereas Mr. William Pynchon, Jehu Burr, and Henry Smith, have constantly continued to prosecute the same, at greate charges, and at greate personal adventure, therefore, it is mutually agreed, that fourty acres of meddowe, lying on the south of End brooke, under a hill side, shall belonge to the said partys free from all charges forever. That is to say twenty akers, to Mr. William Pynchon, and his heyres and assigns forever, and ten akers to Jehue Burr, and ten akers to Henry Smith, and to their heyres and assigns forever, which said forty akers is not disposed to them as any allotment of towne lands; but they are to have their accommodations in all other places notwithstanding.

"10ly. That whereas a house was built at a common charge which cost £6 and also the Indians demand a grate some, to bye their right, in the said lands, and also a greate shallope, which was requisite for the first planting, the value of which engagements, is to be borne by each inhabitant, at theyre first entrance, as they shall be rated by us till the said disbursements shall be satisfyed, or else in case the said howse and boat be not so satisfyed for; then so much meddow to be sett out, about the said howse as may countervayle the sayd extraordinary charge.

"11ly. It is agreed that no man except Mr. William Pynchon shall have above ten acres for his house lot.

"12ly. Anulled.

"13ly. Whereas there are two Cowe pastures, the one lying towards Dorchester, and the other Northward, from End brooke. It is agreed that both these pastures shall not be fed at once;

but that the time shall be ordered by us in the disposing of it for tymes and seasons, till it be lotted out and fenced in severalty.

"14ly. May 16, 1636. It is agreed that after this day, wee shall observe this rule, about dividing of planting ground, and meddowe, in all planting ground, to regard chiefly, persons, who are most apt to use such ground. And in all meddowe, and pasture, to regard chiefly, cattel and estate, because estate is like to be improved in cattel and such ground is aptest for their use. And yet wee agree that no person, that is master of a lott, though he hath not cattel, shall have less than three acres, of planting ground, and none that have cowes, steeres, or year olds, shall have under one acre a piece, and all horses, not less than four akers, and this order in dividing meddow by cattell, to take place the last of May next, soe that all cattayle that, then appeare, and all estates, that shall then truly appeare, at £20, a Cow shall have this proportion in the medowe, on Agawam side, and in the large meadow, Masacksiek, and in the other long meddowe called Nayas, and in the pasture at the north end of the town called End brook.

"15ly. It is ordered that for the disposinge of the hassaky marish, and the granting of homelots, these five men undernamed, or theyre Deputys, are appoynted, to have full power, namely, Mr. Pynchon, Mr. Michell, Jehue Burr, William Blake, Henry Smith.

"It is ordered that William Blake, shall have sixteen polle, in bredth for his homelott, and all the marsh in bredth abuttinge at the end of it, to the next highland, and three acres more in some other place.

"Next the lott of William Blake, Northward lys the lot of Thomas Woodford, being twelve polls broade, and all the marish before it to the upland. Next the lott of Thomas Woodford lys the lott of Thomas Ufford. beinge fourteen rod broade, and all the marish before it to the upland. Next the lot of Thomas Ufford. lyes the lott of Henry Smith, being twenty rod in breadth, and all the marish before it. and to run up in the upland on the other side to make up his upland lott ten acres.

"Next the lott of Henry Smith lyes the lott of Jehue Burr, being twenty rods in breadth, and all the marish in bredth abuttinge, at the end of it, and as much upland ground on the other side as shall make up his lott ten acres.

" Next the lott of Jehue Burr, lyes the lot of Mr. William Pynchon, beinge thirty rod in bredth, and all the marish at the east end of it, and an addition, at the further end, of as much marish, as make the whole twenty foure acres; and as much upland adjoining. as makes the former howse lott, thirty acres in all togeather fifty fowre acres.

" Next the lott of Mr. Pynchon lyes the lott of John Cabel, fowreteene rod, in breadth, and fowre acres and halfe of marish at the end of his lott.

" Next the lott of John Cable, lys the lott of John Reader, beinge twelve rod in breadth and fowre acres and a halfe in marish at the fore end of his homelot.

" The lotts of Mr. Matthew Michell, Samuel Butterfield, Edmund Wood, and Jonas Wood, are ordered to lye, adjoining to mill brooke, the whole being to the number of twenty-five acres, to begin three of them on the greate river, and the fowrth on the other side of the small river.

" It is ordered that for all highways, that shall be thought necessary, by the five men, above named, they shall have liberty and power, to lay them out, when they shall see meete, though it be at the end of mens lotts, giveing them alowance for so much ground.

" We testifie to the order abovesaid being all of the first adventurers and undertakers for this Plantation.

William Pynchon
Mr. Michell   the mark T of Thomas Afford
Henry Smith
the mark of Jehue Burr / John Cabel
William Blake

Edmund Wood

B.

The trial of this lawsuit is recorded in William Pynchon's private book containing his memoranda of such matters as came under his cognizance as a magistrate.

"November 14, 1639. A meetinge to order some Towne affaires & to try causes by Jury.

The Jury. Henry Smyth Henry Gregory Jo: Leonard Jo: Searle Samuell Hubbard Samuell Wright

The Action. John Woodcoke complaines against Jo Cable in an action of the case for wages due to him for certaine work he did to a house that was built on Agawam side for the Plantation.

The Verdict. The Jury findes for the defendant: But withall they find the promise that Jo Cable made to the plaintife to see him paid for his work firme & good. But as for the 5 dayes in coming up with John Cable we find them not due to be paid for he came not up purposely but in his coming he aimed at a lott wch end of his he did attain. Moreover we agree that Jo Cable is ingaged to the plaintif for work don about the house: yet we also judge that Jo Woodcoke is fully satisfied in regard he hath had the use of the ould [Indian?] ground & of the house all that sommer as far as Jo Cable had himselfe."

C.

February the 14th 1638

We the Inhabitantes of Agaam uppon Quinnetticot takinge into consideration the manifould inconveniences that may fall uppon us for want of some fit magistracy amonge us: Beinge now by Godes providence fallen into the line of the Massachusett jurisdiction: & it beinge farr of to repayer thither in such cases of iustice as may often fall out amonge us doe therefore thinke it meete by a generall consent & vote to ordaine (till we receive further directions from the generall court in the Massachuset Bay) Mr. William Pynchon to execute the office of a magistrate in this our plantation of Agaam viz

To give oathes to constables or military officers to direct warrantes, both process executions & attachmentes, to heare & examine misdemenours to depose witnesses & uppon proofe of misdemenor to inflict corporall punishment, as whipping stockinge byndinge to the peace, or good behaviour & in some cases to require sureties, & if the offence require to commit to prison & in default of a common prison to commit delinquentes to the charge of some fit person or persons till iustice may be satisfied, also in the Tryall of actions for debt or trespasse, to give oaths, direct juries, depose witnesses take verdictes & keepe Recorde of verdictes, judgmentes executions: & whatever else may tend to the keepinge peace, & the manifestation of our fidellity to the Bay. Jurisdiction & the restraininge of any that shall violate Godes lawes : or lastely whatsoever else may fall within the power of an assistant in the Massachuset.

It is also agreed uppon by a mutuall consent that in case any action of debt or trespasse be to be tryed: seeinge a jury of 12 fit persons cannot be had at present among us : That six persons shall be esteemed & held a sufficient Jury to try any action under the some of Ten pounde till we shall see cause to yᵉ contrary & by common consent shall alter this number of Jurors or shall be otherwise directed from the generall court in the Massachusetts.

D.

The following compilation of the ancient by-laws of the town is taken from the appendix to the address of the late Hon. George Bliss, senior, delivered at the opening of the old town hall in 1828 :

"Febry the 5th 1649

"A copy of such orders as are made and confirmed by the Inhabitants of Springfield the day and year above written.

"1. For the prevention of disorders in puttinge cattell to pasture on the other side of the great river to the prejudice of men's corne; and yet that men may have the benefit of the pasture there, for theyre cattell in seasonable tyme. It is therefore ordered, that no person shall put over any cattell on the other side of the great river to Pasture there, until the 15th day of October yearly, and from thence untill the eighth day of March they may continue there, by which day the fields there are to be cleared of cattell of all sorts, and if any cattell shall be found there going at liberty, and not under the hand of a keeper, or in an inclosed piece of ground, before or after the days abovesayd, the owners of the said cattell shall be lyable to a fine of 12d. a head for all that shall be found within a 100 rodd of any corne or meddowe, one halfe of the fine to the informer, and ye other halfe to the towne, and shall make goode whatever damadge shall appeare to be done by theyre said cattell in that tyme.

"2. Whereas the planting of Indian corne in the meddows and swamps on the other side of *Agawam* river, hath occationed a long stay after mowing tyme, before men can put theyre cattell thither to pasture. Therefore it is ordered (with the consent of all those that have planting ground there), that no more Indian corn shall be planted there, either in the meddows or swamps, that soe the cattell that have allotments there may be put over by the 15th day of September yearly, provided they take a sure course to prevent theyre cattell from goinge over the river, either by fencing, or a keeper in the day tyme, and by securing them in some inclosure in the night. But there is liberty, for calves to be put over thither, by the 14th of August. And in case any person shall put cattell there before the day expressed, he shall forfeit 2s. 6d. by the head for every such default, and also be lyable to pay all damadge that his cattell shall doe on either side of the river. [This order was soon changed, and the same rule adopted as in the first regulation.]

"3. It is ordered that if any Inhabitant shall desire to make a Cannoe, he may have liberty to fell any tree or trees in the towne commons, and make it or them into Cannoes for his own use, or the use of any Inhabitant. But no such inhabitant shall have liberty to sell or in any kinde to pass away any Cannoe soe made out of the towne, untill it be full five years old, or if he lend his cannoe, it shall be returned within a month. And in case any shall transgress this order, he shall be lyable to a penalty of 20s. for every default.

"4. It is ordered, that whosoever, shall take away or make use of any mans Cannoe without his leave shall forfeit unto the owner 2s. 6d. for every such default.*

*These regulations as to *canoes*, were important, as they were the vehicles in which the farmers every day went from one part of their farms to another.

"5. It is ordered that there shall be no barns or howseing built or set up in the highway betwixt the streete fence and the brooke, except there be soe much room as they can leave 4 rod for the streete or highway, and then men may make use of that side, next the brooke, for what building they please. And if any shall transgress this order, it shall be lawfull for the selectmen to appoynt men to pull downe and demolish such building.

"6. For the prevention of sundry evills, that May befall this Township, through ill disposed persons, that may thrust themselves in amongst us, agaynst the likinge and consent of the generality of the inhabitants, or select Townsmen, by purchasing a lott, or place of habitation, &c. It is therefore ordered and declared, that no inhabitant shall sell or in any kind pass away his house lot or any part of it or any other of his allotments to any stranger, before he have made the select Townsmen, acquainted, who his chapman is, and they accordingly allow of his admission, under penalty of paying twenty shillings for every parcell of land so sold, or forfeitinge his land soe sould or passed away. But if the select Townsmen see grounde to disalowe of the admission of the said chapman, then the toun, or Inhabitants shall have 30 days tyme to resolve whither they will buy the said allottments, which said alottments they may buy, as indifferent partys shall apprise them. But in case the Inhabitants shall delay to make a purchase of the said lands above 30 days after the propounding of it to the select Tounsmen, then the said seller shall have his liberty to take his chapman and such chapman or stranger shall be esteemed as entertained and alowed of by the toune as an Inhabitant.

"7. It is ordered, that, if any man of this township, or any proprietor of land here, or any that shall or may dispose of land here, shall under the colour of friendship, or any other ways, entertaine any person or persons here, to abide as inmates, or shall subdivide their howse lotts, to entertaine them as tenants or other ways for a longer time than one month, or 30 days, without the consent or allowance of the select Tounsmen, (children or servants of the family that remain single persons excepted,) shall forfeit for the first default 20s. to the Towne and alsoe he shall forfeite 20s. per month, for every month that any such person or persons shall soe

continue in this Township without the consent of the select Tounsmen ; and if in tyime of their abode after the limitation abovesaid,
they shall neede relief, not beinge able to maintaine themselves,
then he or they, that entertained such persons, shall be lyable to
be rated by the selectmen, for the reliefe and maintenance of the
said party or partys, so entertained, as they in their discretion
shall judge meete.

"8. For the regulating of workmens and labourers wages. It
is ordered. 1. That all workmen shall worke the whole day,
allowing convenient tyme for food and rest. 2d. Thatt all hus-
bandmen and ordinary labourers from the first day of November
to the first of March shall not take above 16d. by the day wages,
for the other 8 months, they shall not take above 20d. by the
day, except in time of harvest for reaping, and mowing, or for
other extraordinary worke, such as are sufficient workmen are
allowed 2s. pr. day. 3. That, all carpenters, joyners, sawers,
wheelwrights, or such like artificers, from the first day of November to the first of March, shall not take above 20d. pr. day
wages. And, for the other 8 months, not above 2s. pr. day. Tay-
lors, not to exceed 12d. pr. day, throughout the year. 4. That
all teames, consisting of 4 cattell with one man, shall not take
above 6s. a day wages : From May till October, to worke 8 hours
and the other part of the year six houres for theyre days worke.

"And it is further ordered, that whosoever shall, either by
giveing or taking, exceede these rates, he shall be lyable to be
punished by the magistrate, according to the quality and nature
of the offence.

"9. It is ordered, that every householder shall have in a ready-
ness, about his house a *sufficient ladder*, for length suitable to
his howsing, to prevent the danger of fire, on penalty for every
neglect, 5s.

"10. It is ordered, that if any person, shall be taken notice of,
to carry fire in the streete, or from house to house, not being
sufficiently covered, soe as to prevent doinge hurt thereby, he
shall forfeite 5s. for every such offence, proved against him, besides all damages, for what hurt may come thereby.

"11. It is ordered, that if any trees be felled in the common,
having no other worke bestowed on them, above six months, it

shall be lawfull for any man to take them: but any Timber that is cross cutt or fire wood that is cutt out, or set on heaps, or rayles, or clefts or poles, no man may take any of them till they have lyen 18 months after it is so cross cut or cloven. And in case any person shall be found to take away, or convert to his own use, any tymber, or fyrewood, &c., as aforesaid, before the tyme above limited, he shall be liable to make satisfaction to the owner, in kinde, or otherwise, to his content; and shall also forfeite 10s. to the Toune Treasury for every such parcel of tymber, rayles, boltes, or firewood, that he shall soe disorderly take away and convert to his own use. [N. B. This order was in some respects modified in 1660, but substantially continued.]

"12. Whereas, there is observation taken of the scarcity of Tymber about the Toune for buildinge, sawing, shingles, and such like, it is therefore ordered that no person shall henceforth transport, out of the toune to other places any building tymber, bord-loggs, or sawen boards, or planks, or shingle Tymber, or pipe staves which shall be growing in the Toun commons; viz., from Chickuppe river to freshwater brooke, and six miles east from the great river; and, if any man shall be found to transgress this order, he shall be lyable to a fine of 20s. for every freight, or loade, of such Tymber, boards, shingle, or such like, by him soe transported.

"13. To the end that such *candlewood* as lyeth near the Towne may not be wasted by such as burne Tarr, &c., to ye prejudice of the Inhabitants, It is therefore ordered, that no person shall have liberty to gather, or havinge soe gathered to burn any candlewood for the makinge of Tarr, Pitch, or Coale, within the compass of six miles east from the great river, and soe extending from Chickuppe river to the Longmeadow brooke; and if any shall be found to burne any candlewood soe gathered, within the limits or bounds above expressed, he shall forfeite 20s. for every load of candlewood, soe gathered and burnt for Tar, Pitch, or Cole, or ye like use. Provided notwithstanding that every Inhabitant, may gather candlewood for his own family use where he pleaseth.*

---

*This regulation as to candlewood, refers to the state of the plains, and the customs of the people, at that time. By the perishing of old trees, there were, on and in

"14. Whereas it is judged offensive and noisome for flax, and hempe to be watered or washed in or by the brooke, before mens doors which is for ordinary use, for dressinge meate, therefore it is ordered that no person henceforth, shall water or wash any flax or hemp in the said brooke, either on the east or west side of the streete or any where near adjoyninge to it, and if any person shall be found transgressinge herein, he shall be liable to a fine of 6s. 8d. for every such default.

"15. It is ordered that no person shall gather any hopps, that grow in the swamps or any common grounds, untill the fifth day of September yearly, upon payne of forfeitinge what they shall see disorderly gather, and 2s. 6d. for breach of order, the forfeiture to the informer, the 2s. 6d. to the Toune treasurer.

"16. Whereas it is judged needful in sundry respects that each Inhabitant should have the severall parcells of his land recorded, therefore for prevention of future inconveniences, It is ordered, that every particular inhabitant of this township shall repayre to the recorder, that is chosen and appoynted by the toune for that purpose, who, upon information given him by each person of his severall parcells of land, the number of acres, with the length and breadth of ye said alotments, and who are borderinge on each side of him, shall by virtue of his office fairly record each parcell of land, with the limits, bounds and situation thereof in a book for that purpose, for which his pains, the owner of the said lands shall pay unto the Recorder two pence for every parcell of his land, soe recorded. And, if any person shall neglect the recording of his lands longer than six months after ye grant of it, he shall be lyable to a fine of 3s. for every parcell of his land, that is not then recorded; and if after that he shall neglect to record it he shall pay 12d. pr. month for every months neglecte, of any parcell; And auncient grants are all to be recorded by the last of May next upon like penalty.

"17. It is ordered, that if any person, whose houselott lyes inclosed in a general fence, shall desire to inclose a part of it for

the ground, many pine knots, and hearts of trees, which were generally used for torchlights. Formerly it was the custom of the people, to have gathered, every fall, for family use, a quantity of these pine knots, etc. A prudent farmer would almost as soon enter upon the winter without hay, as without pine. This was gathered on all uninclosed land, wherever found.

yards, gardens, or orchard, his neighbour, on each hand of him, shall be compellable to make and sufficiently maintain, the one-half of the said fence from tyme to tyme, provided his share of fence amount not to above ten rods. provided alsoe, that ye said fence exceede not the charge of a sufficient five foot pale, or five rayles. And in case any neighbour shall refuse to doe his share of ye said fence within 3 months after due notice given him of it, he shall be lyable to pay what damadge his neighbour shall sustaine through his default: and alsoe 5s. per month soe long as he shall neglect, for contempt of order.

"18 and 19. [The 18th and 19th are respecting fences, and the oversight and repair of them, and have nothing peculiar in them.]

"20. For the better carryinge on of Toune meetings, it is ordered that whensoever there shall any public notice be given to the Inhabitants by the select Tounsmen, or any other in theyre behalfe, of some necessary occation, wherein the selectmen desire to advise with the Inhabitants, and the day, tyme, and place of meetinge be appoynted, It is expected that all the Inhabitants attend personally such meeting soe appoynted. And, in case the tyme and houre of meetinge be come, though there be but nine of the Inhabitants assembled, it shall be lawfull for them to proceed, in agitation of whatever busyness is there propounded to them, and what the major part of the Assembly there mett shall agree upon. It shall be taken as the act of the whole toune, and binding to all.

"21. The first Tuesday in November yearly [altered afterwards to February,] is mutually agreed on and appoynted to be a general toune meetinge for the choyce of Toune officers, making, continuing and publishing of orders, &c. on which day it is more especially expected that each inhabitant give his personall attendance, and if any shall be absent at the tyme of calling, or absent himself without consent of the major part, he shall be lyable to a fine of 2s. 6d.

"22. It is alsoe ordered, that on the first Tuesday in November, there shall be yearly chosen by the Inhabitants, two wise, discreete men, who shall by virtue of an oath imposed on them by the magistrate for that purpose, faithfully present on the

Court days, all such breaches of Court, or toune orders, or any other misdemenors as shall come to their knowledge, either by their own observation, or by credible information of others, and shall take out process for the appearance of such as are delinquents, or witnesses, to appeare the sayd day; when all such presentments by the sayd partys shall be judicially heard and examined by the magistrate, and warrants for distresses granted for the levying of such fines or penaltys as are annexed to the orders violated, or which shall seem meete and reasonable to the magistrate to impose or inflict according to the nature of the offence. These to stand in this office for a year or till others be chosen in their roome.*

"23. It is ordered and declared, that when any man shall be fairly and clearly chosen to any office, or place of service, in and to the toune, if he shall refuse to accept the place, or shall afterwards neglect to serve in that office to which he shall be chosen, every such person shall pay 20s. fine for refusall to the Toune Treasurer, unless he has served in that office the yeare before; no person being, to be compelled to serve two years together in the same office, except selectmen, two whereof, if chosen againe, are to stand two yeares together; that so, there may be always some of the old selectmen who are acquainted with the Toune affaires, joining with the new.

24.—[Relates to the regulation of swine, and is not necessary to be transcribed. An officer, unusual in later years, was chosen as a general swine ringer, and his fees stated.]

"25. To the end that the common Highways of the Toune may be layed out where they may be most convenient and advantagiose, for the general use of the toune, it is therefore ordered, that the select Tounsmen shall have full power and authority to lay out all common highways for the Toune, where and how they shall judge most convenient and useful for the Inhabitants, though it be through or at the end of mens lotts. Provided, they give them reasonable satisfaction according to equity; but if. the party like not thereof, then it shall be referred to the Judgment of indifferent partys mutually chosen by the partye

---

*These officers, called *presenters*, were chosen for many years. After grand jurors were chosen, they had only town orders to execute.

and the select Tounsmen: and if those two indifferent partys do not agree they shall pitch upon a 3d person to join with them and determine it.

"26. And the Select Tounsmen are alowed liberty to set a certaine toll on carts, that shall pass any highway, which shall appeare more than ordinary chargeable in the reparation of it.

"27. For the equall and indifferent carryinge on and bearinge the charge of makinge and repayreing such common highways and bridges as are, or shall be thought, needful to be made or repayred from tyme to tyme within this township, it is ordered, that every householder. that hath. or keepeth in his use or possession a Teame, consistinge of four cattell, shall on due warninge given him by the surveyor, send at every day and place appoynted his said teame, with his cart and such necessary tooles, as the surveyor shall alowe of, and an able man therewith, to doe such work, as the surveyor shall appoynt him. The like is to be done by those that have but halfe teames. And it is .further ordered, that every other householder, who hath no teame, shall by himself or some other faithful labourer, attend the worke appoynted him by the surveyors, on every day that he shall be called, or required soe to worke. And it is alsoe ordered, that all persons inhabitinge in the toune, who are above £100 estate in other rates, and yet have no teame, every such person shall be compellable to send one sufficient labourer to the highway worke on every day, that he shall be duly warned thereunto, accordinge to his proportion with other men.

"It is alsoe further ordered that every person shall cut downe his stubbs, and cleare the highway before his lott of tymber wood, standing trees, (which are hereby declared to be a mans own,) or any other offensive matter, that the surveyors shall warne him of, within three days after notice given him, or else be lyable to a fine of 12d. for every defect.

"28. Whereas there are surveyors, chosen yearly, for the oversight and amendinge of highways, bridges. and other defects of that nature, that soe the common highways of the Toune may be kept in continuall reparation. To that end, and for the regulatinge of surveyors in the discharge of their office, It is ordered yt ye surveyors for the tyme beinge shall take care, 1. That highways, bridges, wharfs, &c. belonging to theyre care, be made, re-payred, and amended sufficiently, accordinge to theyre discretion, or as they shall be directed by the select Tounsmen. 2. That all highways be kept clear from trees, Timber, wood, earth, stone, or any other offensive matter yt shall annoy the highway, within a mile of any dwelling house. 3. That if any person, upon notice given him by the surveyor, shall neglect to remove or cleare away any such annoyance to the highway, or offensive matter, by him caused, longer than 3 days, then the surveyor shall doe it, and have double recompense for all his labor, cost and charge, from the party so neglecting, besides the 12d. which the party is to pay in way of fine for neglect, according to the order foremen-tioned. 4. That the surveyor shall give three days warninge to such as they call for, and require to come to the highway worke, viz. the day of warning and a day more, soe that men must come the 3d day after warning, unless the surveyors give them longer tyme. 5. That they shall require no householder to worke above 6 days in a yeare, no more of these six days than shall. in a due proportion, fall to his share. 6. That the surveyors shall require no man to worke above two days in a weeke. 7. That they call for these 6 days. for as many of them as shall serve, within the compass of tyme betwixt the 20th of May and 20th of June yearly, and not at any other tyme, unless by the consent of the major part of the select Tounsmen it be agreed unto. and yet, inasmuch as sometimes ways suddenly become defective. that they may not too long be neglected, it is declared that three of ye selectmen meetinge, and any two of them agreeing, may ap-poynt and allow the surveighours to repaire such defective ways. 8. That they duly present to the select Tounsmen all defects of persons, or teames, that, on lawfull warning given, neglect to come to the worke appoynted, who shall give warrant to the con-stable, for present distress, of 2s. fine for a man, and 5s. for a man and teame, to be employed in the next worke that is to be done about highways. 9. That they give in theyre accounts yearly, to the selectmen. at the general meetinge in November, when they yield up their office another yeare."

9

E.

The Indian deed is recorded in these words :

"A coppy of a deed whereby the Indians at Springfield made sale of certaine Lands on both sides the great River at Springfield to William Pynchon Esq & Mr Henry Smith & Jehu Burr for the Town of Springfield forever.

AGAAM

  alias AGAWAM   This fifteenth day of July 1636

It is agreed between Commucke & Matanchan ancient Indians of Agaam for & in the Name of al the other Indians & in particular for & in y° name of Cuttonus the right owner of Agaam & Quana & in the name of his mother Kewenusk the Tamasham or wife of Wenawis & Niarum the wife of Coa, to and with William Pynchon Henry Smith & Jehu Burr, their heires & associates forever, to trucke & sel al that ground & muckeosquittaj or medow accomsick, viz: on the other side of Quana : & al the ground & muckeosquittaj on the side of Agaam except Cottinackeesh or ground that is now planted for ten fatham of wampam, Ten coates, Ten howes, Ten hatchets, & Ten knifes ; and also the said ancient Indians with the consent of the rest & in particular wth the consent of Menis & Wrutherna & Napompenam do trucke & sel to William Pynchon, Henry Smith & Jehu Burr & their successors forever, al that ground on the East side of Quinnecticot River called Usquaiok & Nayasset reaching about four or five miles in Length from the North end of Masaksicke up to Chickuppe River for four fatham of wampam, four coates, four howes, four hatchets, four knifes :   Also the said ancient Indians Doe wth the consent of the other Indians & in particular wth the consent of Machetuhood, Wenepawin & Mohemoos trucke and sel the ground & muckeosquittaj & grounds adjoining, called Masaksicke, for four fatham of wampam, four coates, four hatchets & four howes & four knifes.

And the said Pynchon hath in hand paid the said eighteen fatham of wampam, eighteen coates, 18 hatchets, 18 howes, 18 knifes to the said Commucke & Matanchan & doth further condition wth the s^d Indians that they shal have & enjoy all that Cottinackeesh, or ground that is now planted :   And have liberty to take

Fish & Deer, ground nuts, walnuts akornes & sasachimmosh or a kind of pease. And also if any of o^r cattle spoile their corne, to pay as it is worth : & that hogs shal not goe on the side of Agaam but in akorne time : Also the said Pynchon doth give to Wrutherna, two coates over & above the said particulars expressed, & In witness hereof the two said Indians & the Rest doe set to their hands this p^rsent 15th day of July 1636."

The Indians who signed this deed by making their marks were Menis, Machetuhood, Cuttonus, Kenis, Commucke, Matanchan, Wessaj alias Nepinam, Macossak, Wrutherna, Kockuinek, Winnepawin, Wenawis and Coa.

The clause of attestation is in these words viz. " Witnesse to all wthin exp^resed that they understood al by Ahaughton an Indian of the Massachusett

    JOHN ALLEN
    the marke of
    RICHARD R EVERET   JOSEPH PARSONS

    THOMAS HORTON
    FAITHFUL THAYELER
    the marke of

    JOHN COWNES
    the marke of ⊂⊃ AHAUGHTON

Joseph Parsons a Testimony to this Deed did at the Court at Northampton March 1661 : 62 testify on oath that he was a witnesse to this bargaine between Mr Pynchon &c & the Indians
        as attests ELIZUR HOLYOKE Record^r

July 8. 1679 entered the Records for ye county of Hampshire
        by me JOHN HOLYOKE Record^r "

Then follows this memorandum which is supposed to have been made by John Holyoke.

" Memorandu^m : Agaam or Agawam. It is that meadow on the South of Agawam Riv^r where ye English did first build a house wch now we comonly cal ye house meadow. that piece of ground is it wch ye Indians do call Agawam & y^r ye English kept y^r residence, who first came to settle and plant at Springfield now

so called: & at y⁴ place it was (as is supposed) that this purchase
was made of the Indians. Quana is the middle medow adjoyning to Agawaᵐ or house medow: Masacksick is y⁴ y⁴ English call
the Longmeadow, below Springfield on yᵉ East side of Quin-
ecticot River: Usquaiok is the Mil River wᵗʰ the land adjoyning.
Nayasset is the lands of Three corner meadow & of the Plaine."

F.

                                   Springfield this 5 of the 5 mo. 1648.
Sir,

I received a letter from you with the hands of four magistrates
more to it, to assist two Indians of Quabaug with men, etc., for
the apprehending of three murtherers at Naucotak, which is
about fifteen miles from our town up the river.

These Indians of Quabaug have dealt subtilly in getting Cutshamoquin to get Mr. Eliot to be their mediator to you for the help.
The principal argument which Mr. Eliot doth use to move you is,
that the murthered are your subjects, and thereupon the warrant
from the court runs, that the said Indians may charge either Indians or English to assist them to apprehend them at Naucotak,
1, because the murthered are your subjects, and 2dly, because the
murtherers are within your jurisdiction.

But if things be well examined, I apprehend that neither the
murthered are your subjects, nor yet the murtherers within your
jurisdiction.

I grant they are all within the line of the patent, but yet you
cannot say, that therefore they are your subjects, nor yet within
your jurisdiction, until they have fully subjected themselves to
your government (which I know they have not) and until you
have bought their land; until this be done, they must be esteemed as an independent free people, and so they of Naucotak do
all account themselves. I doubt lest when ours go with strength
of men to disturb their peace at Naucotak, they will take it for
no other than a hostile action; witness their deadly fend which
they have and do bear to the Monaheganicks ever since they took
Sowoquasse from them the last year, which I doubt will be the
ground of a further dangerous war, for I hear that Pacontick will
pursue the quarrell and join with the Indians of the Dutch river
against them. But the Naxicauset must begin the war, and as I

hear either yesterday or this day is like to be the day of fight between them and the Naxicauset; though this river Indians will delay their time till the time that corn begins to be ripe. But now they are making of a very large and a strong fort.

But to return to the case of the murthered. The first three that were murthered the last year lived about six or seven miles on this side Quabaug nearer us, and the murtherers of them are known as they affirm; and there are several small factions of Quabaug, and in all near places there are other small factions. No one faction doth rule all; and one of these petty factions hath made friendship with Cutshamoquin, and that makes Cutshamoquin call them his subjects; but I believe they will stick no longer to him than the sun shines upon him.

The last five that were killed this spring (with one more that escaped) lived in the midway between Quabaug and Nashaway, and yet not properly belonging to either place, but living as neuters, and yet because they were somewhat near neighbors to both places, therefore both places do desire their help against the murtherers. The murtherers of these five are not known; but because the murtherers of the first three are known, therefore they suppose they are the same men. But the man that is escaped saith, that if he can see their faces, he doth know their faces, though he knows not their names.

Mr. Eliot also writ a letter to me to stir me up to assist the said Indians that came from you. 1st. He urgeth me with a command of God to make inquisition for blood, and 2dly with a promise, They shall hear and fear, etc., and hence he concludes that there is no fear of a war to proceed from this dealing.

If the first positions can be made good, namely, that the murthered were your subjects, and 2dly that the murtherers were within your jurisdiction, then Mr. Eliot's exhortation to me had been seasonable, or else not.

But yet notwithstanding I have not declined the business, but have bethought myself how to get it effected in the best manner; and therefore advised the Quabaug Indians to stay until Nippunsit returned from Sowoquasse's house, which I expected within two days, but he came not till the third day. Then we had a private conference, and I ordered my speech thus to him, that I had received letters from you, that whereas Chickwallop desired Cut-

shamoqnin to appoint a meeting at Quabaug, it was your desire
that the meeting might be at Boston, that you might understand
the business as well as the Indian sachems, and that you would
take it kindly, if he would talk with the Naucotak sachems to apprehend the three murtherers, and that they would send some to
the meeting at Boston.

Thereupon Quacunquasit, one of the sachems of Quabaug, and
Nippunsit and others discoursed a long time how to effect this
matter, and who to apprehend in the first place. But neither I
nor my son for want of language could understand their discourse,
but in conclusion they explained unto us what they had concluded
on, namely to take two of the four that were at Naucotak; but
they thought it best not to meddle with Wottowon and Reskes-
coneage, because they were of Pamshad's kindred, who is a Maqua
sachem, but Nippunsit said he would tell him that they should
live hoping he would further them in the taking of the rest; and
all the Indians consented to this motion as the most feasible and
likely way to attain their end in the rest. The other two, namely
Wawhelam and his brother, Nippunsit hath undertaken by some
wile or other to bring them to my house in a private way, and
then he will leave them to me to apprehend them, and so to send
them to you. And this they thought might be effected about ten
or twelve days after this conclusion was made, which was made
two days before the date of this letter.

And thus by these means they will engage the English as the
chiefest parties in their business.

But I must confess I look upon this service in sending them to
you as a difficult and troublesome service, for 1, I have no prison
to keep them safe, and 2dly, it will occasion great resort of Indians to my house to see what I will do with them, and 3dly, we
shall want men; and I perceive that the Indians are afraid to
meddle with them, unless they can make the English the principal in the business.

If the Lord should let loose the reins to their malice, I mean to
their friends and abettors, it may be of ill consequence to the English that intermeddle in their matters by a voluntary rather
[than] by a necessary calling, for they and their friends stand
upon their innocency, and in that respect they threaten to be
avenged on such as lay any hands upon them.

And any place is more obnoxious to their malice than the Bay by far; especially the Naucotak Indians are desperate spirits, for they have their dependence on the Mohawks or Maquas who are the terror of all Indians.

My advice therefore is, that you will as much as may be take the matter from us; which may thus be effected, send three or four men to our plantation with all speed, that may live being here either at the ordinary or at some other house till the said parties be brought to me, if they be not brought before they come. They may improve their time here by doing some work, and if there be not a sufficient number of Indians to go with them to carry them safe, I may appoint more men that the business may not fail for want of a good guard. Let these persons march here [with] a charge to be private and silent in the business till they see it effected. You may send these men away on the second day. If the Indians should make an escape, and not be taken, yet the charge of three or four men in so weighty a business for the fairer carrying of it on, is not to be stood upon. If they be taken, before they come, I will set a guard upon them for two or three days in hope you will send them with as much speed as may be. Indeed there should not be a day's delay after they come to my house. It will prevent the tumult of Indians and prevent their waylaying. If these two be once apprehended and put to death, then they have determined the death of six more near Quabaug, and only the former two to live.

Thus have I as briefly as I can (though abruptly) related the substance of the matter. I entreat you that the men may call to my son Davis for a letter before they come away. They must be active men and light of foot, for the better countenancing of the business. I shall ere long send you further intelligence about this Pacoutuck business with the Monaheganicks. The Lord is able to divert their intentions, though it is to be suspected it is intended for the utter ruin of the Monaheganicks, and the English will, I fear, be embroiled in the war.

Your assured loving brother in the Lord.

W. PYNCHON.

Haste, haste.

For his loving brother, the Dep'u'y
Governor, with speed.

On receipt of this letter, the deputy governour, Dudley, sent it with this address :—

"To his honored friend Mr. John Winthrop, governour, at his house in Boston, deliver it with all speed."

Governour Winthrop writes upon it :—

Sir,

I pray acquaint Mr. Eliot with this letter, and let me have your advice about it speedily. So I rest

Your loving brother,

JOHN WINTHROP, Gov'r.

9 (5) 48.

[It was, we may be sure, sent to Dudley from what here follows on the same paper inside.]

Upon reading this letter and conference with Mr. Elyott I give my advice (which you require) for a pause in the business, before we proceed any further in it.

1. For that the ground and warrant of our meddling in it is by this letter taken away, it being denied that the murthered were our subjects or the murtherers within our jurisdiction.

2. If the murtherers should be apprehended and brought to us, the party escaping is, for ought we yet know, all the witness against them, he affirming he knows their faces, which yet is doubtful, the murther being done in the night.

3. It is like in Mr. Pinchon's opinion to draw a war upon us, which, if (as he saith) it be provoked by us voluntarily, not necessarily, we shall incur blame at home and with our confederate English, and want the [aid?] from heaven in it and comfort in prosecuting it.

4. The charge and difficulty which the sending men out in hay and harvest time would be considered.

5. A pause will advantage us in hearing what the Narragansetts will do upon Uncus whom we must defend.

6. And if so, it cannot be wisdom in us to stir up other Indians against us to join with the Narragansetts.

I have forgotten two other reasons while I was setting down these.

I think a messenger would be despatched to Mr. Pinchon, to

let such Indians loose, if any should be apprehended, which I think will not be, they who have promised not being like to do it, or if Mr. Pinchon see cause to do otherwise, to leave it to him.

THOS. DUDLEY.

G.

Wequogan was one of three Indians, who, in 1674, sold to Elizur Holyoke and others, for the use and behoof of the town, a tract bounded Northerly by "Chickuppe" River, Southerly by the Scantic and Freshwater rivers, and extending from the foot of Wilbraham Mountains on the East, as far as Five Mile pond on the West.

In this sale the previous conveyance made by their "Ancestors" to William Pynchon of the land between this tract and the "River Quinecticut" was recognized and confirmed.

In this sale of 1674, Wequogan is mentioned as formerly called Wrutherna, but probably was not the Indian of that name, who signed the deed to Pynchon in 1636. He may have been his son.

Mr. Haven, in his Historical address delivered at Dedham in 1836, states that, among a small party of Indians, who were killed or captured near that town in a later period of Philip's war, was "the Sachem of the faithless tribe at Springfield." Undoubtedly this was Wequogan.

H.

Right Wor^{pm}

The light of another day hath turnd o^r yesterday fears into certainties and bitter lamentations for ye calamities and distresses of o^r bretheren and ffreinds at Springfield, whose habitations are now become an heape Such increase of judgm^{ts} shows ye greatnesse of ye wrath y^t is kindled against us and ye greatnesse of ye provocations y^t have caused it. We have nothinge to say but that the Lord is righteous & we have rebelled greatly rebelled against him. The inclosed from the Honord Major will give you such account of it as is wth us to mate. We have little more to adde only that the houses standing are about thirteene. Two men and one woman slain. viz. Leift Cooper who was going toward the fort to treate wth the Indians y^t the day before p^{r}tended great ffreindship

10

being wth three or four more gott about a quarter of a mile out of Town was shott so as he fell off his horse; but got up again and rode to the end of ye Town where he was shott again & dyed. The oth^r was one Miller of Springfield. There appeared not (according to their æstimate) above 100 Indians; of whom their own were the cheife. Their old Sachem Wequogan (in whom as much confidence was putt as in any of their Indians) was ringleader in word and deede. Another of their principall men cryed out to them and told them he was one y^t burnt Quabaug and now would make them like to it: They were gone ere Major Pynchon came in with his forces wch was about two or three of ye clocke. They signifyed their sence of his approch by their hoops or watchwords & were p^rsently gone. Major Treate was gate down some hours sooner on ye West side of the River: whose coming being perceived; five men went out of Town and altho pursued by twenty Indians carried over a boate wch was filled wth men but the Indians standing on Rivers banke shott at them & shott one through the necke (who is not like to recover) they durst not adventure to passe ye River. Till Major Pynchon was come in and the Indians gone.

It was but the day before viz on ye 4th of October y^t ye garrison souldiers about 45 in number left them; to their mutuall sorrow as looking they should quickly after be in hazzard of y^t ruine wch is now come upon them.

Our army had p^rpared all things in readinesse to goe forth on Munday at night (wch was ye occasion of calling forth these from Springfeild) against a considerable party discovered about five or six miles from Hadley. But the three alarms we mett wth & ye tydings from Springfeild wholly disappointed it.

O^r men in these Towns, who before trembled at the order, That none should be left in garrison when the army went out; are now much more distressed at the thoughts of it as looking at y^mselves thereby exposed to inevitable ruine upon ye enemies assault wch we must then expect: Especially o^r Town of Hadley is now like to drinke next: (if mercy p^rvent not) of this bitter cup: We are but about 50 families & now left solitary

The neerest Town now left upon the river on this side being (as I guesse) about 70 miles distant. And those on ye other side

the River being so unable to come at us wth any help had they it ;
to afford. Experience shews us that an hundred men on the other
side ye River can lend little releife. We desire to repose o^r confidence in the eternall & living God who is the refuge of his people ; a p^{r}sent one in the time of trouble : and to stand ready to
doe and suffer his will in all things : acquainting yo^{r}selves wth o^r
p^{r}sent state y^t so if there be any thinge y^t yor wisedomes see it to
call for & yo^{r}selves in a capacity to apply it we may not faile
thereof : Perhaps the impowring of some man or men as the
Honord Major or Capt : Appleton or both to direct & order us in
o^r fortifications might *not* be unusefull. We are in the Lords
hands and there we would be keeping his way & doing his
will wthout any amazem^t. Yet the Lords now delivering his own
as well as o^r houses into ye enemies hand is more amazing &
threatning to us. His will be done To his grace I comend you.
And rest

> Yo^r Worps : humbly in all service J^{NO} RUSSELL.

O^r wounded men are greatly distressed for want of Medicines.
Those by sea not yet come at us : those expected by Capt. Waite
left at Roxbury.

I.

Springfeild. Oct. 8. 1675

Honored S^r

I desyred Mr Russell to give yo^u an aco^t of ye sore stroake upon
Pore distressed Springfeild, wch I hope will excuse my late doeing
of it : on ye 4th of oct o^r Soldiers wch were at Springfeild, I had
called all off leaving none to secure ye Towne bec ye comissioners
order was so strict :

That Night Post was sent to us that 500 Indians were about
Springfeild intending to destroy it so y^t ye 5th of oct wth about 200
of o^r Soldiers I marched downe to Springfeild when we found all
in flames about 30 dwelling houses burnt down & 24 o^r 25
Barnes my Corn Mill saw mill & other Buildings : Generally
mens hay and Corne is Burnt & many men whose houses stand
had their goods burnt in other houses wch they had caryd y^m too :
Leivt Cooper & two more slayne & 4 psons wounded 2 of wch are
doubtfull their Recovery. The Ld hath made to drinke deepe of

the Cup of sorrow, I desire we may consider ye opperation of his
hand, & what he speakes yet That ye Town did not utterly perish
is cause of grt Thankfullness: As soone as o^r forces appeared
ye Indians all drew off, so y^t we saw none of y^m: sent out Scouts
y^t Night & ye next day but discovered none, neither can we sat-
tisfie o^rselves wch way they are gon their Tracts being many ways:
som^t we think they are gon downe ye River o^r last discovery was
of a considerable Tract vpward o^r Indeavors here are to secure y^e
houses and corne y^t is left: for this sad pvidence hath obstructed
o^r goeing out wth ye Army & w^t can be done I am at a grt loss:
o^r People are vnder grt discouragem^{ts} Talke of Leaving ye Place,
we need yor orders & direction about it. If it be deserted how
wofully doe we yeild to & Incourage o^r Insolent enymy & how
doth it make way for ye giving vp all ye Townes above: If it be
held it must be by strength and many soldiers, & how to haue
Provision I meane Bread for want of a Mill is difficult: ye soldiers here already complaine on y^t aco^t although we have flesh
enough: & this very straite I mean no Mill will drive many of
o^r Inhabitants away especially those y^t have noe Corne, & many
of them noe houses wch fills & throngs vp every Roome of those
y^t have, together wth ye soldiers now (wch yet we cannot be wthout)
increasing o^r Numbers: so y^t indeed It Is very vncomfortable
Living here, & for my owne pticular it were far better for me to
goe away bec here I have not anything Left I meane noe Corne
neither Indian nor English & noe meanes to keepe one beast here
nor can I have Releife in this Towne, because so many are destitute: But I resolve to attend what God calls me to, & to stick
to it as long as I can & though I have such grt loss of my Comforts
yet to doe what I can for defending ye Place. I hope God will
make vp in himselfe what is wanting in ye creature to mee & to
vs all: This day a Post is sent vp from Hartford to call off Major
Treate wth a pt of his soldiers: from Intelligence they have of a
pty of Indians lying ag^t wethersfeild on East side of ye river so y^t
matters of action here doe Linger exceedingly wch makes me won-
der what ye Ld intends wth his people strange Providences divert-
ing vs in all o^r hopefull designes: & ye Ld giving opportunity to
ye enymy to doe vs mischeife & then hiding of y^m And answering
all o^r Prayers by Terrible things in righteousness. S^r I am not

Capable of holding any Comand being more & more vnfit & almost Confounded in my vnderstanding: the Ld direct you to Pitch on a meeter pson then ever I was: according to Liberty from ye Councell I shall devolve all vpon Capt Appleton vnless Major Treate returne againe till yo shall give yor orders as shall be most meete to yor selves:

To speake my thoughts all these Townes ought to be Garrisoned, as I have formerly hinted & had I bin left to my selfe I should I think have done yt wch Posibly might have pvented this damage But ye express order to doe as I did, was by ye wise disposeing hand of God who knew jt best for vs, & therein we must acquiess And truly to goe out after ye Indians in ye swamps & thickets is to hassard all or men vnless we knew where they keepe: wch is altogether vnknown to vs, & God hides from vs for ends best knowne to himselfe I have many tymes thought yt ye winter were ye tyme to fall on ym but there are such difficultys yt I shall leave it yet suggest it to consideration, I will not further Trouble yo at psent but earnestly crave yor Prayers for ye Lds vndertaking for vs & sanctifiing all his stroakes to vs: I remaine   yor vnworthy servt

JOHN PYNCHON.

We are in grt hassard if we doe but str out for wood to be shot downe by some sculking Indians. Mr Glover had all his Bookes Burnt: not so much as a Bible saved: agrt loss for he had some choise Bookes & many:

K.

NOTE.—The following correspondence of Capt. Appleton is taken from a printed copy, in which the original spelling has been modernized. The same thing is true also of the letter of William Pynchon to Gov. Dudley. Appendix F.

Council of Massachusetts to Captain Samuel Appleton.

Capt. Appleton.—The Council have seriously considered the earnest desire of Major Pincheon, and the great affliction upon him and his family, and have at last consented to his request to dismiss him from the chief command of the army in these parts, and have thought meet upon mature thought to commit the chief command unto yourself, being persuaded that God hath endowed you with a spirit and ability to manage that affair, and for the better enabling you to your employ, we have sent the council's

order enclosed to Major Pynchcon to be given you ; and we refer
you to the instructions given him, for your directions ordering you
from time to time to give us advice of all occurrences; and if you
need any further orders and instructions, they shall be given you
as the matter shall require. So committing you to the Lord, de-
siring his presence with you, and blessing upon you, we remain

> Your friends and Servants.

Boston, 4th of October, 1675.

   Capt. Samuel Appleton
Commander in chief at the
   head quarters at Hadley.

Capt. Appleton, to Governor Leverett, Oct. 12th 1675.

Right Worshipful :

Yours by Lieut. Upham I received, as also that of Oct. 9th
from you, together with the order from the Commissioners, concerning the number and order of management of the forces in
these parts. In reference whereto, I humbly present two things
to your consideration; First, as to the ordering the chief command to one of such an inferior capacity ; the very thoughts of it
were and are to me such matter of trouble and humiliation, as
that I know not how to induce my spirit to any compliance
therewith, lest, it should prove a matter of detriment and not help
to the public, from which nothing should have moved me but the
consideration of the present exigencies, together with the remembrance of the duty I owe to you and the common concerns ; unto
which the Hon. Major having added his sorrowful complaints, for
which there was such abundant and manifest cause. It was indeed an heart-breaking thing to me, and forced me against my
own spirit to yield to the improvement of the whole of my small
talent in your service, until I might send to you (which I now do)
to intreat that there may be speedily an appointment of some
other, more able to the work, and likely to obtain the desired end.
I humbly intreat your most serious consideration and help herein.

Secondly, my humble request is, that you would be pleased to
revise that part of your work, and the Hon. Commissioners' orders, which doth strictly prohibit the fixing of any of our soldiers

in garrison. I doubt not but the reasons inducing thereto were weighty, which notwithstanding we find the attendance here extremely hazardous to the loss of towns (which is the loss of all) as appears both by lamentable experience we have had at Springfield, as also what is obvious to the eye of each man's reason. The thought hereof put us to great straits, most willingly would we attend the express letter of your order, and yet cannot but tremble at the thought of exposing the towns to ruin. Be pleased as seasonably as may be, to give us your resolve herein.

As to the state of poor desolate Springfield, to whose relief we came (though with a march that had put all our men into a most violent sweat, and was more than they could well bear) too late, their condition is indeed most afflicted, there being about 33 houses and twenty five barns burnt, and about fifteen houses left unburnt; the people are full of fear, and staggering in their thoughts as to their keeping or leaving of the place. They whose houses and provisions are consumed, incline to leave the place, as thinking they can better labor for a living in places of less danger, than where they now are; hence seem unwilling to stay, except they might freely share in the corn and provision which is remaining and preserved by the sword. I cannot but think it conducive to the public (and for aught I see, to the private) interests that the place be kept, there being corn and provisions enough and to spare for the sustenance of the persons, whose number is considerable, and cannot be maintained elsewhere, without more than almost any place can afford to their relief. The worth of the place is also considerable, and the holding of it will give encouragement and help to others, and the quitting of it great discouragement, and hazard to our passage from one place to another, it being so vast a distance from Hadley to any other town on this side the River. I have in regard of ye present distress of ye poor people, adventured to leave Capt. Sill there, to be ordered by the Hon. Major until further order be received. What hazard I run, I am not insensible, but do rather choose to adventure hazard to myself than to the public, and so throw myself on your worship's mercy in so doing.

We are at present in a broken posture, incapable of any great action, by reason of Major Treat's absence, who upon a report of

Indians lower down the river about Hartford, was (while I was absent) recalled by the Council of Connecticut, upon the eighth of this instant, and is not yet returned, nor do I know how it is with him, nor when he is like to return. We have sent to the Council of Connecticut signifying that our Colony having been mindful to complete their numbers, we do earnestly expect and intreat his speedy return, and that the ammunition now at Hartford, and needed by us, may be brought up under their guard, hereto we have not yet received answer.

In the account of Springfield houses, we only presented the number of them on the east side of the river, and that in the town platt; for in all on the west side and in the out-skirts on the east side, there are about sixty houses standing, and much corn in and about them; which coming into the Indian's hands will yield great support to them. We have been considering the making of a boat or boats, and find it not desirable; first, because the river is not navigable, and so none made here can be had up. Secondly, should we make any above the falls, there must be an army to guard the workmen in the work:—Thirdly, we find exceeding hard, by any provision, to secure our men in the boats, by reason that the high banks of the river giving the enemy so great advantage of shooting downward upon us. And lastly, as we must follow the enemy where he will go, we must either leave a very strong guard upon our boats, or lose them perhaps as soon as made, there being now come in sixty men under Captain and Lieut. Upham, and we needing commanders, especially part of our men being now at Springfield, and we not daring to send all thither, we have retained Capt. Pool to command these sixty men until further orders be given.

We are but this evening come up from Springfield, and are applying ourselves presently to the sending out scouts for the discovery of the enemy; that so the Lord assisting, we may with these forces that we have, be making some onset upon him, to do something for the glory of God and release of his distressed people, the sense of which is so much upon my heart, that I count not my life too dear to venture in any motion wherein I can persuade myself I may be in a way of his providence, and expect his gracious presence, without which all our endeavors are in vain.

We confide, we shall not, we cannot fail of ye steady and continued lifting up the hands and hearts of all God's precious ones, that our Israel may in his time prevail against this cursed Amalek; against whom I believe the Lord will have war forever, until he have destroyed him. With him I desire to leave ourselves, and all the concern, and so doing to remain

Your servant obliged to duty,

SAMUEL APPLETON.

I communicated thoughts with Major Pynchon about the garrison placing at Brookfield. And although it would be some relief and comfort to our messengers going post, yet considering the great charge which must necessarily be expended upon it, and that they have no winter provision there for the keeping of horses, without much use of which we see not how they can subsist; we have not seen cause to order any garrison thither, (nor for aught yet appears shall do, except we have some special direction from you for it.) We also find that these three towns* being but small, and having sustained much loss in their crop by reason of the war, and had much expense of what hath been gathered here both by the soldiers and by those coming to them from the places that are already deserted,† are like to find the weight of sustaining the army too hard for them; and therefore we apprehend it will be advisable and necessary to send to Connecticut to afford some help as may be needed from some of their plantations.

Capt. Mosely makes present of his humble service to your worship, whereto the scribe also desires to subjoin the tender of his own.

These for the Worshipful John Leverett, Esq. Governor of the Massachusetts, at Boston.

Capt. Appleton to Governor Leverett.

HADLEY, Oct. 17, 1675.

Right Worshipful :—

I thought it convenient and necessary to give you a present account of our state and posture, that so you might thereby be the

---

*Hadley, Hatfield and Northampton.
†Deerfield and Northfield.

11

better capacitated both to send orders to us, and to know how to
act towards others, as the case doth require.

On Tuesday, Oct. 12th, we left Springfield, and came that
night to Hadley. On the 13th and 14th, we used all diligence to
make discovery of the enemy by scouts ; but by reason of the distance of the way from here to Squakaheage,* and the timorous-
ness of the scouts, it turned to little account; thereupon I found
it very difficult to know what to do. Major Treat was gone from
us, and when like to return we knew not ; our orders were to
leave no more in garrison, but keep all for a field army, which
was to expose the towns to manifest hazard. To sit still and do
nothing, is to tire ourselves, and spoil our soldiers, and to ruin
the country by the insupportable burden and charge. All things
laid together, I thought it best to go forth after the enemy with
our present forces. This once resolved, I sent forth warrants on
the 14th inst. early in the morning to Capt. Mosely and Capt. (as
he is called) Seely, at Hatfield and Northampton, to repair forth-
with to the head quarters, that we might be ready for service.
Capt. Mosely was accordingly with us with his whole company,
very speedily. Capt. Seely† after a considerable time, came
without his company, excused their absence by his want of commission. This commission he produced, and upon debate about
it, seemed satisfied, expressing that his purpose was to attend any
orders that should be given. I wrote another warrant and gave
into his hand to appear with his company, which are about 50
men, the next morning ; but in the night he sent a messenger to
me with a note, about intelligence from Major Treat to stay till
further orders, &c. I presently posted away letters to the Council at Hartford, declaring to them how the work was obstructed
by absence of Major Treat, (whose company indeed I much
desired, he approving himself while with us a worthy gentleman,
and a discreet and encouraging commander,) and by absence (indeed) of Capt. Seely and those few that were with him. The
copy of my letter to the Council, and of my warrant to Capt.
Seely, and his returns to me, I send you here all of them enclosed.

—

*Northfield.

†Captain Seely was stationed at Northampton with a company of Connecticut troops.

This morning, Oct. 16th, I received a letter sent first to Major Pynchon, and from Springfield hither, from the Council at Hartford, dated Oct. 12th, which I also send the copy of, whereby you will perceive that they seem to make some excuse, and stick at the want of forces here from Plymouth, wherein I am not so fitted to return them an answer as perhaps I might be, for want of understanding the specialities of agreement between the Hon'd Commissioners of the United Colonies; only thus much seems evident, that they all agreed their number should be 500, the which is made up by our Colony and Connecticut, though there be none from Plymouth, so that we see the reality of the thing is done, though we know not the reason of Plymouth not bearing a share in it. By a letter from Major Pynchon, we understand that the ammunition is come up to Springfield, which I am presently sending for. This likewise informs of an old Indian Squaw taken at Springfield, who tells that the Indians who burnt that town, lodged about six miles off the Town ; some men went forth, found 24 fires and some plunder. She saith there came of the enemy, 270. That the enemy in all are 600. The place where they keep is at Coassit, (as is supposed) about 50 miles above Hadley.

After the sending my letter to Hartford, I drew forth our own men all but Capt. Sill's (who are near sixty) intending to march up to Sqhakeage; we had not marched above a mile or two, ere we received intelligence by post, that the enemy was by his tracks discovered to be in great numbers, on the west side of the river. We presently changed our course, and hasted over the river. It was after sunset ere we got out of Hatfield. We marched some miles, and in the dark saw a gun fired, and heard its report ; and our scouts saw and heard this gun. Some also said they heard a noise of Indians. My purpose was now to march to Deerfield; but, upon what we discovered, our officers especially Capt. Mosely, was very apprehensive of danger to the towns here, if we should march up. This being often pressed, and I alone for proceeding, none of Connecticut men with us, nor any left in the towns of Hadley and Hatfield, and night threatening rain and tempest, I yielded against my own inclinations to return to our quarters, which we did in the night.—This morning, we understand by scouts, that there is certainly a great number of the enemy at Deerfield, and some of them much nearer. This evening, we have received a letter from the General Court at Hartford, whereby I perceive it is very uncertain when we are like to have their forces again. In very truth, I am in straits on every side. To leave the towns without any help, is to leave them to apparent ruin. To supply with any, except now in the absence of Connecticut, is hardly reconcileable with the order of the commissioners.—This evening late, I am assaulted with vehement and affectionate request from Northampton (who have already with them about 50 of Capt. Seely's men) that I would afford them a little more help, they fearing to be assaulted presently. And, at the same time while these are speaking, Capt. Mosely informs, the enemy is this evening discovered within a mile of Hatfield; and that he verily expects to be assaulted there to-morrow, which I am so sensible of, that I account it my duty presently to repair thither, now at ten or eleven of the clock in the night, some of the forces having already passed the River. Nor are we without apprehension of Hatfield and Hadley's danger at the same time, where with respect to the wounded men & the town, I strive with myself to leave about twenty men, or but few more, though the Indians were yesterday discovered within 5 or 6 miles; and we are necessitated to send so many of them for posts (on which account six are at this present) & other occasions as makes them less than their little selves. I desire in all to approve myself to the Lord, and faithfully to his peoples interest, so as I persuade myself would most reach and take your hearts, were you present. I crave your candid acceptance of what comes from a heart devoted to your service ; and your speedy reasonable return to what I have written, which waiting for, I leave the whole matter with the wise ordering, and remain

Your Worship's most humble servant

Samuel Appleton.

Hoping for the return of our post from you, and that our going forth last night, might produce something of consequence we delayed the sending away this letter one day. But Providence hath delayed our expectation and desire in both. Our post is not come in, and we have wearied ourselves with a tedious night and morning's march, without making any discovery of the enemy.—Thus the Lord orders all things wisely, holily, well; may we but see, and close with the goodness of his will, and wait for the working of all things together, it shall be peace, in the latter end, to all that love God, that are perfect ones, for which praying and waiting, I am

your servant as above
Oct. 17th afternoon.   S. A.

These for the worshipful John Leverett Esq Governor of the Massachusetts, in Boston—
Hast—Hast—Post-hast.

NOTE.—An attack was made upon Hatfield on the 19th Oct. by 7 or 800 Indians, which was repulsed with little loss. See Hubbard for particulars—he adds, "Major Appletons Sargent was mortally wounded just by his side, another bullet passing through his own hair, by that whisper telling him how very near death was, but did him no other harm."

West Springfield Centennial.

1774-1874.

WITH PORTRAITS AND ILLUSTRATIONS.

AN ACCOUNT OF THE

Centennial Celebration

OF THE

TOWN OF WEST SPRINGFIELD, MASS.,

WEDNESDAY, MARCH 25, 1874.

WITH THE

HISTORICAL ADDRESS

OF THOMAS E. VERMILYE, D. D., LL. D.

POEM: By Mrs. Ellen P. Champion.

AND OTHER FACTS AND SPEECHES.

Compiled by J. N. BAGG, with an APPENDIX, containing Genealogies
of the Bagg, Ashley, Champion, Chapin, Cooley, Day, Ely,
Lathrop, Parsons, Rogers, Smith, Stebbins, Wade,
White, and Bliss Families.

8vo.—Cloth, pp. 141.   Price, $1.00.

Historical Works, Published and for Sale by F. W Morris, Springfield, Mass.

BI-CENTENNIAL OF WESTFIELD.

1669-1869.

THE WESTFIELD JUBILEE.

The Celebration at Westfield, Mass.,

ON THE TWO HUNDREDTH ANNIVERSARY OF THE INCORPORATION OF
THE TOWN, OCTOBER 6, 1869, WITH THE

HISTORICAL ADDRESS OF THE HON. WM. G. BATES,

And other Speeches and Poems of the occasion, with an APPENDIX, containing Historical Documents of local interest.

WESTFIELD, MASS., 1870.   8vo. Cloth.—pp. 226—Price, $1.25,

Bi-Centennial of Hadley.

1659-1859.

Celebration of the Two Hundredth Anniversary

OF THE

Settlement of Hadley, Massachusetts,

AT HADLEY, JUNE 8, 1859.

WITH HISTORICAL ADDRESS,

By REV. PROF. F. D. HUNTINGTON, D. D.

POEM, - - BY EDWARD C. PORTER, A. B.

And the other exercises of the occasion.

NORTHAMPTON, 1859.

8vo.—pp. 98.   Paper, 75 cts.   Cloth, $1.00.

HISTORY

OF

WESTERN MASSACHUSETTS,

THE COUNTIES OF

Hampden, Hampshire, Franklin and Berkshire,

EMBRACING AN

Outline or General History of the section, an account of its Scientific aspects and leading interests, and separate histories of its one hundred towns.

By JOSIAH GILBERT HOLLAND.

Three Parts In Two Volumes.

Cloth—pp. 1139, with Map—Price, $4.50.

HISTORY

OF

Amherst College,

DURING ITS

FIRST HALF CENTURY.

1821-1871.

BY W. S. TYLER,

Of the Class of 1830,

Williston Professor of the Greek Language and Literature.

Illustrated with numerous Steel and Wood Engravings.
Royal Octavo—Cloth, pp. 671—Price, $5.00.